this book will change your life

amanda weaver

Entangled Publishing, LLC
2614 South Timberline Road
Suite 109
Fort Collins, CO 80525
Visit our website at www.entangledpublishing.com.

Embrace is an imprint of Entangled Publishing, LLC.

Edited by Stephen Morgan & Ava Jae
Cover design by LJ Anderson and Heather Howland
Cover art from Shutterstock

Manufactured in the United States of America

First Edition September 2015

embrace

For Matt and Lily, always.

For Matt and Lily, always.

Chapter One

HANNAH

Eighteen: the number for Argon on the periodic table, the third most common gas on Earth.

Eighteen: the number of freshmen who were admitted into the Honors Chemistry Program this year.

Eighteen: the score I got on my first test in Honors Chemistry I.

That's eighteen out of thirty-four, so it's more than half right, but it's only fifty-three percent, so yeah, it's pretty bad. I've been staring at it for the past hour and a half, trying to figure out what I did wrong.

I mean, the red pen scribbled all over my paper *shows* what I did wrong, but why did I freeze up during the test? Why did I make such stupid errors? I know this stuff— Or at least, I thought I did, so why did I bomb my very first college test in my best subject?

I've been closed up in the library all morning, staring at my disastrous test while the rest of the campus enjoys their Saturday in beautiful Arlington. The letters and numbers are starting to blur together on the page. I can't take it anymore. I need to get out of here, take a breath, maybe take a walk downtown.

Ten minutes outside and the first raindrop hits me square on the nose— I'm in trouble. As in, I have a twenty-minute walk to my dorm, and my umbrella is still somewhere in the vacuum under my bed. I don't even have time to hope the clouds will hold back long enough for me to run back, because not half a step later the sky opens up.

It's a biblical downpour; big fat drops fall so close together it's like standing in a shower. Rain hits the ground so hard it bounces back up, soaking my shoes in dirty backsplash. I plaster myself against the brick building, but the tiny carved wooden eaves two stories up don't do a thing to shield me. This isn't working. I have to get inside.

I duck into the nearest shop, through an old-fashioned glass-paned door painted with the name "Prometheus Books" and stop, sputtering and dripping rain onto the dull wood plank floor. I'm in a small, quiet bookstore that smells like ink and paper. This place seems familiar. I think I've walked past here before, but I've never stepped inside.

A big square counter on a low platform sits near the front of the room. There might be a cash register on it, but it's hard to tell because it's stacked with books. More books are stacked on the floor all around it, leaning precariously, about ready to topple over. Up front, the shelves are only waist-high, so the windows facing the street are visible. The rain is still coming down so hard I can't see the other side of the road.

Air conditioning breathes over me, chilling my wet skin. I shiver and cross my arms over my shirt, which is plastered to my chest like a second skin.

"That's some downpour." A woman steps out from behind a bookshelf a few feet away and smiles at me before turning back to the shelf. She's probably in her sixties, but she's dressed like a hippie with a brightly colored patchwork blouse to her knees, loose pants, and a long, silver braid.

She cranes her head back as she reads the titles on the shelf from underneath red, funky glasses connected to a beaded chain around her neck.

"Yeah, I wasn't expecting that."

"They didn't say rain in the forecast this morning," she says. Big silver and turquoise bracelets slide up her wrist as she slips a book into place onto the shelf. She turns, this time ducking her chin to look at me over the glasses. Does she ever look at anything *through* the lenses?

"Might as well have a look around while you wait it out." She smiles. I return the smile awkwardly and wipe my damp hands on my jeans.

As much as I'd prefer to go back to my dorm room and brood over my bad grade, she's right. The rain's only getting worse. Like it or not, I'm stuck here for the foreseeable future.

The store is small and made smaller by the bookshelves reaching to the ceiling. They line the room, rows of them running the length of the store, front-to-back. They're all full—overflowing, really—with books.

With a sigh, I turn back to explore the store. Where to even start? A handwritten index card is taped to the end of each shelf, identifying what's on it—philosophy, science, western history (Europe 900 to 1900), western history (modern Europe)... I work my way around the room, past literature, popular fiction, romance, science fiction, mystery, biographies, and politics. On the right side of the store, there's a wooden staircase leading to a half-floor above, like a loft.

"Hobbies and popular culture upstairs. Children's books, too," the woman calls from the depths of the shelves. How did she even know I was over here? Creepy.

Stacks of books on each step lean against the wall all the way up. I pause halfway up the stairs on the landing, crouch, and run my fingers over the dusty spines.

"Those aren't shelved yet," says a deep male voice behind me. "But if you're looking for something specific, I can help you find it."

I spin around to a guy sitting on a stool behind a square counter several feet away. I hadn't even noticed him until he spoke because he's half buried behind stacks of books. The blue glow of a computer screen in front of him glints off his glasses, making it hard to see his eyes.

I take a shaky breath and try to look normal. *Books. I'm in a bookstore. Forget the stupid quiz.*

I hadn't planned on buying anything, but maybe I should. He and the lady have both been really friendly. Loitering in their store to avoid the rain and then leaving without buying something would be rude, right? Except I have no idea what to get.

I shrug, my gaze running around the room, all the shelves, all the books. "Just looking for a book, I guess." Looking for a book. In a bookstore. Where they sell books. Genius.

He chuckles and looks at me for the first time. He has

a nice smile. "Well, you're in the right place. What kind of book?"

I shrug again. "Um… I'm not sure?"

His dark, heavy eyebrows arch up behind his glasses. "Well, what do you like to read?"

My face goes warm again. "I'm not…much of a reader, I guess."

A pause. "Not much of a reader?" He frowns, like the very idea is incomprehensible. I've probably just offended him or something. Come to think of it, saying, "I'm not much of a reader" in a bookstore is kind of like swearing in church.

"I'm a chemistry major," I offer by way of explanation.

He pushes back from the computer. He's younger than I thought at first, probably also a student. Thin, with a mess of thick, dark brown hair that looks like it's trying to fight its way off his head. He's wearing a faded navy hoodie over a gray T-shirt. The glasses are black framed, a little angular, and emphasize his high cheekbones and his furrowed eyebrows.

He's cute, in a bookish kind of way, which is perfect, considering he's literally surrounded by them. He looks as much a part of this store as the books.

"Sooo…" he says slowly. "Let's start at the beginning. Fiction or non-fiction?"

"Either. Fiction, I guess." I can't remember the last time I read something that wasn't for school.

"Fiction." He pinches his bottom lip between his thumb and forefinger. He's got long fingers and nice hands. His wrists where his hoodie sleeves have pulled back are weirdly elegant, and his lips are a little full for his face. He pushes his glasses up the bridge of his nose. "And you really don't read?

For fun?" His eyes are brown—dark brown—with really thick, dark lashes. I'm officially ogling him now.

Oh. He's expecting an answer. I wish I *could* say I was a voracious reader just so I could talk to him about books. I don't know why I don't read. I guess with science stuff taking up all my time—clubs, internships, homework—I never made it a priority. I shake my head in response.

"Wow, this is a challenge." He slides out from behind the counter. "Follow me."

He heads toward the back of the store, down an aisle between shelves, where I passed all the novels earlier. Maybe they have a book about a girl who implodes her first semester in college. So much promise. So much potential. Then... nothing.

I cringe. *Happy thoughts. Focus on happy thoughts.*

Like Bookish Boy. He's taller than I would have guessed—maybe six feet—but it's a lanky, unimposing height. His hoodie clings to his shoulders and upper arms. The points of his collarbone where they join his shoulders and the angles of his shoulder blades across his back poke through the fabric. But he doesn't look bony, only spare. Lean.

He stops at the back wall, his eyes scanning rows of books. He runs his long fingers through that unruly mop of dark hair and clenches and unclenches his fingers. My stomach clenches and unclenches with him. I can't stop staring at him. He's just so...so...

"So a book. And you don't read," he murmurs. He pulls one from the shelf, then shakes his head and puts it back. He does the same with another, muttering the whole time. "Dickens? No, absolutely not. You'd never read again. Let's

see…probably something modern…"

He's so absolutely focused on the books. It's like the only thing in his world right now. I should say something, engage him in conversation so I'm not just a hopeless girl who doesn't read. "What's your favorite book? Maybe I'll start there?"

He throws his head back and laughs. I smile— He has a great laugh. "Oh God, my favorite? That's like… That's *impossible.* There's no way to have just *one* favorite book."

"Why not? Which one did you like the best?"

He looks at me, and my stomach plunges like I've fallen off a Ferris wheel, and I'm on the long, blind, breathless drop toward the ground. He's so cute. *So* cute.

"I love different books for different things. One book might make me think about something in a way I never have before. Another might make me feel something new. So which is better, thinking or feeling?"

He's waiting for me to answer, but I can't because I've never thought about it before, and his smile is kind of distracting, so I just shake my head.

"Exactly. There's no one answer. No absolute. In a way, I love every book I've ever read because I took something from every one. Except *The Red Badge of Courage.* I really hated that one. Utterly irredeemable. But this isn't about me. This is about you and the book you haven't read yet…" He arches an eyebrow expectantly.

"Hannah."

"Hannah. This is about the books *Hannah* hasn't read yet."

"That would be pretty much all of them, except the ones I had to read for English class."

He shakes his head. "Tragic. Okay, so what to read first? God, a person could go crazy trying to choose." He ambles down the shelves, pulls books out, debates their merits and puts them back.

Finally, he hands me a book. "I'm not sure yet, but hang on to that one. It's a possibility." Then he hands me another. "This one, too. Wait. No, never mind." He takes it back, re-shelves it, and moves on. Every few minutes a book makes the "maybe" cut and adds to my growing pile.

I glance at the titles. What's in each one that he's considering? They all mean so much to him. These books suddenly seem like windows to alternate universes, places he's been to and remembers. Places I want to go.

Ten minutes and a ten-book stack later, he stops and examines the pile. Some he discards. "Thomas Pynchon for a neophyte. What was I thinking?" he mutters, setting the book aside.

After a couple more minutes of sorting, he smiles triumphantly and picks up a book. "Okay. Maybe this one." He looks at the book, then at me, and his smile gets even bigger. "Definitely this one. This book will change your life."

I arch an eyebrow. "A book will change my life?"

"Any book can change your life if it's the right book and if you let it. Every book *can* change your life."

I turn it over in my hands. *The Book Thief.*

"I thought about Austen, but it's been done to death, and you'll find that on your own eventually. There's always *To Kill A Mockingbird*, but that's probably the one book you *have* read, in like ninth grade or something. At least, you'd better have or your English teacher should be fired." He rubs his eyebrow with his thumb and pushes his glasses back up his nose. It's adorable. "So yeah, *The Book Thief*. Serious, literary, but still very approachable. History you're already familiar with, a young heroine, solid supporting characters, *and* there's some good thematic stuff that kind of applies to your situation. So... We'll see."

"Wow. That's a lot in one book."

He shoots me a quelling look. I get the feeling that picking this book out for me is the most exciting thing he's done today. His enthusiasm is contagious and—kind of miraculously—I'm desperate to start reading. I want to see all those things he's seen in it.

"You have to come back when you finish," he says over his shoulder as he leads me back toward the register. "I want to hear what you think about it. I'll even give you a discount, but you have to promise to come back and tell me about the book."

"I'll come back as soon as I finish." I have to summon my courage for the next thing I say, because flirting with guys is *definitely* not my thing, especially cute guys I just met. My heart thrums, but thankfully, my voice comes out normal. "When do you work? So I know you'll be here?"

"Oh, I'm here all the time. All weekend and most afternoons. And I'm Ben, by the way."

Ben. That's a great name. *Ben*. He told me his name. And he asked me *my* name. It feels like I've got champagne bubbles in my veins, making me float a few inches above the ground.

"Okay, Ben." I finish paying for the book. "I guess I'll see you around."

His smile is lopsided; the left corner hikes up, and his eyes go a little crinkly. That smile tingles all the way to my toes. "See you around, Hannah."

My stomach flips right over when he says my name.

The downpour has stopped as abruptly as it started, leaving the outside world dripping and soggy, and me with no reason to linger any longer in Prometheus Books. It's time to go. But I'm coming back. He asked me to come back, and there's no way I won't.

"See you," I say with a little awkward wave, clutching my book to my chest. The bell over the door rings behind me, and I turn just as another customer comes in, one he knows because he greets her by name.

"Hey, Alex," Ben says behind me. "Looks like you just missed the rain."

I don't hear what the girl says as the door closes behind me. I glance back through the glass and catch one more glimpse of Ben, smiling adorably and talking to the new customer, before I turn and hurry back toward campus. I can't wait to start reading.

Chapter Two

Wow. Okay, so Hannah's cute. Gorgeous might be the right word. Normally, I'd roll my eyes at someone who says they've never read a book they weren't assigned in school, but she was so eager that it was kind of…charming.

I'm still watching her leave, still off-kilter from the whole encounter when the bell over the front door rings and in comes another customer. Except it's not just any customer. It's Alex.

Alex and I have been dancing around each other for nearly a year now, ever since she started working at the coffee place across the street. I keep thinking it's inevitable that we'll end up together, but months have gone by and we're still not.

"Hey, Ben!" she says as she crosses to the register.

I straighten and smile. Alex always looks pretty without

even trying. Her long, dark brown hair is up in a ponytail, she's barely wearing any makeup, and she looks great. She sets a coffee cup in front of me.

"A bribe," she says. "I need you to dig *The Pelican Brief* out of this mess for me. I know you've got a copy somewhere."

I wince internally. Grisham? Really? Okay, so maybe we don't like the same books, but I'm not going to give her grief about her love of lurid legal dramas. Everybody's got a guilty pleasure.

"You didn't have to do that. It's my job to find books for people."

"Yeah, yeah, but us customer service drones have to take care of each other, right? God knows nobody else will." Alex is a senior, like me, but unlike me, she hates her job at Coffee Oasis. "Rough day at the Oasis?"

"Looks like you had your hands full yourself with that wide-eyed kid I saw leaving."

For some odd reason, that makes me bristle slightly. "Nah, she was all right. I liked her." That's a pretty tepid description considering how much fun I had while she was here. Picking out that book for her was the most enjoyable thing I've done all week.

"Well, lucky you. You would not *believe* this woman who came in this morning." She props an elbow onto the counter and angles her long, lithe body to the side, settling in to vent about her day. We do this a lot. "So there are a dozen people in line because, *hello*, it's a Saturday. She takes ten minutes to read the menu and asks all these ridiculous questions before she finally orders four salted caramel lattes. The line is out the door by the time I finish making them, and *then* she flips out because I didn't use soymilk she didn't ask for.

Ugh. I can't wait until I'm through law school, and I never have to wait on anyone again."

Alex and I are friends partly because we're both students, working part-time jobs on this same commercial strip, and partly because we're both going to law school next year. Maybe. Alex is seriously gung-ho about it. Me? Not so much. I envy her certainty. I wish I could want it the way she does.

She's beautiful, smart, and acing all her pre-law classes. My dad would die of happiness if I brought Alex home to meet the family; she's everything they'd ever want for me. I *do* genuinely like her, but every time I try to work up the nerve to ask her out, the words get stuck in my throat. For all the time we've spent swapping stories from retail hell, I can't tell if she sees me as anything more than a friend. I think she does, but it's been nearly a year, and I'm still not sure what I want from Alex.

"Wow, sounds like a nightmare."

"You have no idea. So, you think you can find the book before my break is over?"

"You seriously underestimate my skills, Alex." I slide out from behind the register. "It just so happens I know exactly where your book is."

She laughs and follows me back into the stacks. Sure enough, the copy of *The Pelican Brief* is right where I expected to find it.

"You're like the book savant, Ben."

I'm not sure if that's a compliment or not, but I decide to take it as one. "This place only looks like chaos. I've got it all up here." I tap my temple.

"That skill will serve you well in law school."

I scowl. "Right. Law school."

"How much do I owe you?" she asks, not noticing my grimace.

I wave her off. "Consider it a trade. I was coming over for a coffee later anyway."

"You sure?"

"Absolutely."

"Thanks!"

I leave Alex browsing through the rest of the Grishams and head back to the register, surreptitiously watching her while I work. She's hot by anyone's estimation. Smart, ambitious, and we've got the law school thing in common— This should be a no-brainer. So why am I still stalling?

"Ben, did you catalog this one yet?" Adele's voice startles me out of my Alex fixation.

"That's supposed to be in modern philosophy."

Adele smiles and shakes her head. "You've got every book in this store in that head of yours. Who needs a computer when we've got you here?"

"Not every book. Not when Ralph keeps dragging more in every day."

Ah, Ralph, the owner of Prometheus Books. As fearless a leader as he is an old grump.

Ralph loves books, but he doesn't like dealing with customers. Or people in general. So he works a couple hours in the morning, when almost no one comes in, and then he takes off and goes scrounging for more inventory, even though we're out of space. I work when I'm not in class, and Adele, Elliot, and me—mainly Adele and me—actually run the place.

Adele hesitates. "How do you think she'll enjoy her book?"

"She loves those law dramas. She'll probably like that one, too."

"Not Alex. The other girl. The wet one."

The wet one? My heart skips a beat as I put two and two together. "Oh, you mean non-reader Hannah." That's a good question— Will she even read *The Book Thief* I gave her? Will she ever turn back up and tell me what she thought of it? She was freaking adorable when I gave it to her... I hope she keeps her promise.

"I guess we'll find out," I say. "She said she'd come back and tell me about it."

Adele glances at Alex and smiles a little. "Maybe." Then she drifts off into the stacks with her book.

Alex lingers for a while longer, long enough for the coffee she brought me to get cold. Finally, she heads back toward the door.

"Break's over." She sighs. "Back to the grindstone."

I smile in sympathy, but it's different for me. The truth is, I'd probably be hanging out in Prometheus all weekend even if I didn't work here. "Hang in there. Try not to kill anyone."

"No promises." She winks. "Have a good weekend."

The weekend— Here's my opening. If I'm ever going to man up and ask her out, this would be the perfect time. I could ask her about her weekend plans, suggest we do something together. But when I open my mouth, my throat closes up, and I make a strangled little sound instead of actual words.

Jesus, I'm hopeless. I try again, but Alex is nearly out the door, so I end up just waving with my mouth half open. Brilliant. A year of this and I still can't manage to get it done. I drop my head down onto my arms and groan. Hell, I couldn't even manage to flirt with Hannah, who didn't even make me nervous.

My future's basically been planned out for me, and while my dad hasn't been so old-fashioned as to pick out my girlfriend for me, I have to admit, she's perfect for the job. So why am I hesitating? What's wrong with me? And why am I thinking about that girl Hannah when I just let the perfect girl walk away from me yet again?

Chapter Three

HANNAH

A good student would go back to the library and study for chem, but I don't. I go straight back to my dorm, lie on my bed, and read. I leave the lights off, reading by the soft glow of the twinkle lights strung over my bed, getting lost in the German village in the book.

Hours later, the door opens and the overhead light flips on, making me startle and blink. I feel like I've been in a cave for years.

Jasmine stands just inside the door, staring at me. On your average Saturday in the dorms, everyone shuffles around in tank tops and pajama pants, hair in uncombed, messy ponytails. Not Jasmine. Her brown skin glows against her yellow sundress, and her strappy wedge sandals make her legs look crazy long. Perfect, as always.

I have no idea where she's been all day. She always has

these incredible plans, like a celebrity slumming it in disguise as a college student. Was she ever disappointed she got paired with a quiet chemistry major for a roommate? She never acts like it, even though we're from separate planets.

"Sorry, were you sleeping?"

Rubbing my eyes, I sit up. "No, reading. Wow, I lost track of time."

"Reading? Is that what you're doing to avoid chem now?"

My stomach churns— My test is wadded up and waiting for me at the bottom of my backpack. But I can't think about that yet. I'm not ready to face it again.

"No, I just got this book today downtown, and I got really caught up in it."

"At World of Books?" she asks, referring to the monster chain bookstore near campus.

"No, Prometheus Books. It's all used stuff. Do you know it?"

Jasmine wrinkles her nose. "What were you doing in that place?"

"I got caught in the rain. But it's cool inside. The staff is really helpful and friendly." My gaze drops to my quilt, and I'm working the edge of my paperback, hoping I'm not blushing. My pale skin is a dead giveaway when I'm embarrassed about something.

"Oh, the *staff* is really *helpful*, huh?" Jasmine laughs, totally on to me.

My face goes hot. Shit. I'm totally blushing. "Okay, there was a guy."

"A guy."

"A cute guy."

"Mmm-hmm." Jasmine drops her oversized bag onto

her desk chair and flops onto her bed, facing me. "Describe the cute guy, please."

"I don't know. Bookish. Kind of geeky. Tall, dark hair. Glasses."

"Glasses? Lord, cute boys in glasses are my kryptonite." Jasmine sighs.

"I know, right? The glasses actually made him cuter. I don't get it."

"Glasses are magic."

"Seriously."

"So did you talk to this cute boy in glasses or did you just check him out from behind a stack of books?"

Ugh. It's embarrassing how accurately Jasmine is describing my modus operandi. I mean, I'm not completely socially dysfunctional. I dated a few boys in high school. Okay, I dated *two* boys in high school who I met through science camp. I've never just randomly met a guy on the street. Or in a bookstore. But at least I did decently well this time. I think.

"No, we talked. His name is Ben. He picked out this book for me."

"Ah, so you dropped everything to read it."

"It's a good book."

Jasmine holds up her hands. "Hey, who can resist a cute boy in glasses? I'd have done the same." She hesitates. "What about your chem test?"

I groan and flop back onto my bed. "Don't remind me."

"Have you told your dad?"

My eyes widen. "No! Absolutely not."

"Maybe you should," Jasmine says gently. "He's a chemist, Hannah. I'm sure he's been there."

I cover my face with my hands. "No, he'd never

understand how I could bomb so badly on my very first test. I don't want to disappoint him."

"I'm sure you're just adjusting and—"

"I know… He warned me about all that before I came. I've been a big fish in a small pond all my life, and now I'm the little fish. I'm not the teacher's darling anymore. I know."

What I don't say is that my dad wouldn't be mad. Mad would be manageable. He'd be *sad*. Disappointed. Worried. And that's *so much worse*. We lost my mom to cancer when I was ten, so my dad and I are really close. But even more than that: Dad and I are so alike, and science is the biggest thing we have in common. We've been doing experiments together since I was four. Science is *us*. It's the language we speak to each other.

How can I tell him that the first time I tackled it alone, I failed? It's like I failed him, too. I've failed *us*. I can't tell him— I *won't* tell him. I just have to fix this. Maybe college has thrown me more than I expected, but I'm ready for this. I've spent my whole life preparing for this moment. I just need to regroup and try again.

Tomorrow. I'll try again tomorrow. But tonight I'm going to read *The Book Thief*.

Jasmine sighs. "If you're sure."

"Yeah, I was just having an off day or something. My first college test. I'm sure I'll be okay next time."

"Sure you will. Did you eat yet?"

Eat? I've done nothing for hours and hours but read, lost in Liesel's world as it falls apart. I haven't eaten anything since breakfast, and now that she mentions it— "I'm starving."

"Come on, then." Jasmine grabs my hand. "Your book

boy will still like you if you take a break for dinner."

I laugh and follow her out of our room and down to the dining hall. But I stay up until four in the morning that night, reading Ben's book.

Chapter Four

"Jesus, what did Elliot do in here?" I'm trying to make sense of this inventory entry, and I just can't. Nothing in the computer adds up.

"Don't ask me." Adele brushes past the register with another stack of books. "I don't understand any of that."

Elliot works two afternoons a week, barely part-time. He should not have access to the inventory database, because all he does is fuck stuff up. I've tried explaining this to Ralph, but he doesn't get it. Frankly, Ralph shouldn't have access to the database, either— He's even more hopeless than Elliot. But thankfully, Ralph is a technophobe and rarely logs on, so it's not a problem.

Elliot, meanwhile, spends his shifts dicking around on Facebook, then feels obliged to hop over into the inventory and do stuff, so it looks like he's been busy. All he does is make more work for me, and it's not like I'm some genius at this stuff. Words are my comfort zone, not databases.

"Hey!"

I look up so quickly I practically give myself whiplash. It's a girl's voice—my heart beats a mile a minute—but it's not Alex. It's cute non-reader Hannah.

She's smiling ear to ear as she leans forward on the counter, and I'm smiling, too. I don't know why I'm smiling. I probably look like an idiot. Shit. Say something. Say something smart.

"Oh, hey. You came back," I manage. I think I sound normal. God, what's wrong with me today?

She bounces on her toes and grins. It's fucking adorable. "You told me to."

I chuckle. "I know. Did you read it?"

Her big doll eyes widen. She bites her bottom lip and nods— And then she starts *crying*. Well, not like weeping or anything, but her eyes well up and tears catch in her crazy-long lashes. She looks like Bambi standing there, all teary and blinking. I have this insane impulse to run my thumbs under her eyes to wipe the tears away.

"It was…*amazing*." She swipes at her cheeks and cradles the book against her chest. "Sorry. I don't know why I'm crying. I thought I got it all out of my system when I was reading, but I guess not."

I smile. "So I take it that means you liked it?"

Her breath comes out in a long, wavering sigh. "Liked it? That feels so small for how I felt when I finished. It was beautiful, and horrible, and I loved it, and couldn't bear to keep reading and…yeah. A book really can be all that stuff at once. You were right."

I'm grinning at her by the end of her little speech. When she showed up here last week, she'd never read a book for fun. Now she's having this emotional breakdown about one. I did that. I gave her that experience, and it feels amazing.

I wave my hand at the room around her. "And you're just getting started."

She smiles back. "I feel just like Liesel. Actually, I feel *awful*. She fought for every word she could get her hands on, and here I am surrounded by all this, and I didn't even care."

"You're a college kid from Ohio, not an orphan in Nazi Germany. Don't be too hard on yourself."

"Still, it feels entitled. I can't believe I took all this for granted." Her conviction kills me, like she's determined to read as much as she can because Liesel couldn't. My fellow lit majors can get so caught up in their heads when they talk about books, trying to one-up each other with cleverness or cynicism. Few are this genuine, this un-ironic, this purely enthusiastic. And none of them are this cute. Hell, she's making me want to read *The Book Thief* all over again.

"Okay, fine," I say. "You're everything that's wrong with today's youth because you don't read."

"I *didn't* read. Now I do. So what should I read next?"

"That's as big a question as what to read first. Come to the back. This will take some time." I hop out from behind the counter and lead her toward fiction in the back of the store. I'm buzzing with anticipation— Doing this last week was so fun, and now I get to do it again.

My head spins with all the classics she should read. I mean, if we're just talking about the western canon we could be here all day, but that might be overload. She should probably stick to contemporary for now, and even then, nothing too out there. I'm not going to dump *Finnegan's Wake* in her lap just yet. Baby steps.

"Hey, Adele," I call out as we go. "Keep an eye on the register, okay?"

"Got it." Her disembodied voice floats back from somewhere in the store.

"Does she own Prometheus?" Hannah whispers.

"Adele? No, she just works here. Maybe. Well, I'm not exactly sure of her employment status. She might be paid. Or maybe she's just sleeping with the owner, Ralph. I've never asked. She's just here all the time."

"Like you."

"Yeah, but I'm paid, at least nominally, and definitely *not* sleeping with Ralph."

Hannah laughs. She looks so serious, but her laugh transforms her face. Her eyes light up, and she glows with it.

"Are you a student?" she asks.

"Yep. Senior year."

"What's your major?"

"English Lit, as crazy as that is."

"Why is that crazy?" That little furrowed line appears between her eyebrows. "It's obvious you love books."

I shrug and peruse the shelves. "Can't get rich with an English degree. At least not if you ask my dad."

"Well, what do you want to do?"

I hesitate. This is where I'm supposed to say "law school," but I don't. For some reason, the truth pops out. "Grad school."

"Yeah?"

"Yeah. The head of the English department here is amazing." Again, I find myself oversharing, telling her something

I haven't said out loud to anyone. Maybe it's because she's a stranger, so it's not so scary to be honest. I've got nothing to lose. "I'd love to stay on and get my master's under him. Maybe go for my PhD, too. But... It won't happen."

"What would you do with a master's? I mean, once you're out of school?"

I grimace. "Teach, which I know is crazy."

"Why is that crazy? It sounds perfect for you."

I smile at her. "You barely know me."

Her giant Bambi eyes go wide and she blushes. "It-it just seems so obvious," she stammers. "Even meeting you once. You're so smart, and you know so much about books. You make everything sound interesting. I think you'd make an amazing teacher."

Jesus, *I* might be blushing after that. Nobody's ever described me that way. I've never told anybody about that dream because I figured they'd roll their eyes and laugh. But just for a second, I can imagine myself really going for it—standing in front of a class of college students and discussing the complicated layers of literature.

But that's just a fantasy. I live in reality.

"Well, not everybody thinks so." I pass her another book. "Here, this one's a maybe. What about you?"

She turns the book around to look at the title. "Me, what?"

"Chemistry, right? That's a pretty significant major."

She looks pleasantly surprised. "Wow, you remembered? Honors Chem, actually."

Whoa. Pretty and wicked smart, too? "Seriously? Are you some sort of savant or something?"

"No, I just had really good grades in high school. Why?"

I glance at her and lift a shoulder. "You just seem so

young. Like, too young to even be in college."

She bristles like a puffed up kitten. "I'm eighteen. A freshman. I'm not *that* much of a freak." She must catch grief about her age all the time because it's clearly a sore spot.

"Never said you were. I just thought girls liked hearing they look young."

"I get carded going into R-rated movies."

Ouch. I laugh. "Okay, got it. Here, hold this one, too."

She's quiet for a minute as I scan the shelves, debating the options. Gabriel García Márquez? Maybe…Graham Greene? That might be good. It's been ages since I've read Greene.

"Is that one good?"

I start. "Hmm?"

She looks from me to the book in my hand, smiling and eager to read.

"Oh, no, I was thinking I wanted to read this again." I sigh. "I want to read them *all* again. There are too many books and not enough hours in the day. Do you feel like that about science? Like there's just not enough time to do everything you want to do?"

The light in Hannah's eyes dims a little, and her gaze drops. "Well, sure, I guess. My program's really competitive, and I want to do well. You have to be dedicated, right?"

That's not what I meant, but I just smile and shrug. "Sure. So let's figure out what you're going to read next."

"Which one of those is your favorite?" she asks impatiently. "Just give me that one."

She motions to the Greene, but I hold it up out of her reach. "I told you, it doesn't work like that. You're on a book high. This is almost harder than picking your first book.

What if I give you the wrong book now? What if it bores you, or it isn't as good as the last book? Then that's it. You'll never come back to get another book."

Hannah smiles and her whole face lights up again. A guy could get addicted to that smile. "I promise you I'm coming back." Pink flares in her cheeks again, and she hooks her hair behind her ears. "So which book?"

It takes me another half hour to decide. While I debate the various merits of the choices at hand, we walk around the store, and I point out other books she should read, if she had all the time in the world. A couple of customers come in, but Hannah doesn't leave, hanging out unobtrusively by the register while I ring people up. It's nice to have her there, chatting excitedly about the possibilities for her next read.

"Okay," I tell her when the last customer clears out. "This is the one. The next book that changes your life."

I slide it across the counter to her.

"*A Prayer for Owen Meany*. Is it about religion?"

"No, not really. There's some spirituality in there, but as a theme. It's not a polemic. It's just… It's hard to explain. But listen, give me your phone. I want you to text me when you get to Owen and tell me what you think."

"My phone?" She digs it out of her bag and passes it over to me. I enter my number into her contacts.

"Promise you'll text me. Owen is the best part. You'll see."

"You want me to text you?"

I can't help but smile. She sounds excited— Honestly, I am, too. I haven't had this much fun talking about books in ages. I really hope she doesn't forget. I don't want to wait another week to talk to her again. "Yeah, sure."

Hannah grins and puts her phone away. "Okay, I will."

"Promise?" I give her hand a little nudge with mine. She blushes. Damn, she's adorable— That blush will be the end of me.

"Yeah, I promise."

"And you'll come back next week for another book?"

She looks right into my eyes, and my stomach drops. "I promise," she says.

Hannah tucks the book into her bag like it's precious, smiles at me one last time, and heads out. I'm still blinking at the spot where she stood, not sure what just happened. I can't remember the last time I felt this way, a little light-headed and stunned. It's nearly closing already. Somehow half my workday slipped past while I was talking with Hannah.

"Who was that?" Apparently, my roommate John came in as Hannah was going out. He looks back over his shoulder as she disappears down the sidewalk.

"That's Hannah. Get this, she *doesn't really read*."

John fakes a gasp and claps a hand to his chest. "You're flirting with a girl who doesn't read? Are you feeling okay?"

My face goes hot. "Shut up. I wasn't flirting with her."

"Mmm-hmm."

"Seriously, she's a freshman."

"So? Still eighteen. And my friend, that was definitely flirting."

I bite my lip. He has a point, I guess. I'm only twenty-one myself, older than her, but not that much. And I'm pretty sure we *were* flirting at the end there. But why would I do that? I don't have room in my life for that. "Whatever. You know my situation."

John rolls his eyes. "You mean your hopeless crush on

Alex?"

I groan. "Why did I ever tell you about that? And who said it's hopeless? She brings me coffee every time she comes in."

"You don't even like coffee."

"It's the thought that counts."

"So? Ask her out already if you're so into her."

"I'm choosing my moment."

John laughs. "You've been choosing your moment for nearly a year. Pretty sure a thousand of them have already passed you by."

"What's your point?"

John shrugs. "Maybe if it was meant to happen, it would have happened already."

"You're an astrophysicist. Why are you mouthing off about fate?"

"This isn't science. It's dating. And it's pretty simple. Boy meets girl—"

"Girl is *perfect* for boy."

John chuckles. "If you say so."

"She is." John opens his mouth to argue, but I cut him off. "So are you here just to bust my ass or did you want something?"

"Beer," he says. "I want beer. Come with me to get some."

John and I were paired up randomly in the dorms freshman year, but we're a pretty good fit, so we moved to an off-campus apartment sophomore year and have been together ever since. He's an astrophysics major, but not nearly as serious and dry as that makes him sound. He's way more laid-back than me and funnier, and the easy-going demeanor is deceptive.

Most people have no idea how smart he is. Hell, I've been living with him for three years and sometimes I forget. Then he'll drop some fact in conversation, or I'll catch a glimpse of his homework and remember I'm friends with a young Einstein. He's freakishly smart, the kind of smart that can coast through four years of astrophysics with a 4.0 and nearly no effort.

I bet John won't break an intellectual sweat in school until he's well into his PhD. Sometimes I suspect that when he's forty, John will unleash some theorem upon the world that will change humankind's understanding of time and space, and he will have worked it out on the back of an envelope while he was watching *Breaking Bad*. He'll publish the book that changes everything, and then he'll order a pizza.

"So?" John prompts. "Beer? Baseball? You in?"

I hesitate. "I don't know. Where do you want to go?"

John's not into the whole college bar scene, and neither am I. He hates those loud beer-and-cheap-shots places near campus nearly as much as I do.

"I'm just heading to Smitty's." He shrugs. "Nothing fancy. The Reds/Braves game starts in an hour."

Smitty's is okay. It's on the edge of the downtown district, too old and uncool to be popular with the frat crowd. It's mostly locals and the oddball college students like John and me. Since I've yet again failed to ask Alex out, cold beers and the Reds in the playoffs sounds great. Then I'll go home and read, and I absolutely will not wait for Hannah to text me.

Chapter Five

Hannah: *Hi, it's Hannah. I just got to Owen. Why is everything capitalized?*

Ben: *That's how he talks.*

Hannah: *He talks in all caps?*

Ben: *He says in the book that his voice sounds different.*

Hannah: *But it's just capitalized letters. What does that sound like?*

Ben: *What do you think it sounds like? What do you*

hear in your head when you read it?

Ben: *Hannah?*

Ben: *Are you still reading?*

Ben: *Hannah?*

Hannah: *Oh. OH!*

Hannah: *I love this book!*

Hannah: *Was it all really predestined, do you think?*

Ben: *Owen and the kids? Maybe Owen's the only one who knows for sure.*

Hannah: *But*

"*Why* are you smiling like a crazy person, Hannah?"

I jump and drop my phone in mid-reply. "What? Nothing. I was just sending a text."

Jasmine crosses her arms over her chest and stares me down. "Texting your dad? Your friend Samantha back home?"

I roll my eyes. "I was texting Ben."

"*Bookstore* Ben?" She grins. "You guys are texting now? When did it escalate to texting?"

"This past weekend. He gave me his number."

"Ooooh, this sounds good."

"Not like that. He gave me another book to read and wanted me to text him when I got to a certain part to tell him what I thought. We've been texting about the book since then. That's all."

"Well, okay then."

I should ask Jasmine for advice about Ben. I'm so out of my depth with him. I like him. I *really* like him. I'm more excited talking to Ben about a book than I ever felt with Scott, my boyfriend for most of senior year.

Scott was nice, but during the first week here at Arlington State, a bunch of girls on our floor got drunk, and everybody shared how far they'd gone and with how many guys. When they got to me, for just a split second, I *forgot* I'd lost my virginity to Scott. I'm pretty sure that's not how it's supposed to be. There's something better out there, and I want to find it. Now I think I know who I want to find it with.

"Is that good?" I blurt out. "That he wanted me to text him?"

"It's not bad. It'd be better if he was calling you to go out, but it could be worse. He hasn't texted you pictures of his junk or anything, right?" She cranes her neck to look at my phone.

I laugh and hide it under my leg. *"No.* There are no junk pictures involved. Just words. Not the least bit dirty." *Sadly.*

She hums, poking through the overloaded tray of jewelry on her dresser, looking for the mate to her earring. She's getting ready to go out. Of course. "All right. At least he has manners."

"It's just… I like him. A lot."

Jasmine chuckles. "Yeah, I can tell. Just let it happen the way it happens. Sounds like you guys are off to a good start."

My face warms as I smile. "I hope so."

"So, now on to the important stuff. How do I look?"

She spins around and strikes a pose. She looks amazing, of course.

"You look great. Where are you going? It's Tuesday."

"A team thing with Sean."

Jasmine and Sean have been dating since high school. She's a serious business major, but she came to Arlington State because he's on the football team here, and she wanted to be near him. He's kind of a big deal on campus, but you'd never know it seeing him with Jasmine. He worships her.

She smooths her hair again and slicks on some more lip gloss. "Have fun with your texting date!" And then she's gone.

I've just settled back down with *Owen Meany* when my phone buzzes under my thigh. The caller ID pops up, and my breath catches in my throat. It's Ben. *Calling* me.

"Hey." It's a miracle I sound so nonchalant, because I sure don't feel it. My palms are sweating, and I'm so giddy I could bounce on the bed.

"Hey, you quit texting in the middle of an important part. Are you still reading?"

"Oh, sorry, my roommate, Jasmine, was talking to me. She just left. Something with her boyfriend Sean's team."

"What team?"

"Football."

"Wait. Sean Jackson?"

"You know him?"

Ben chuckles. "I know *of* him. Everybody knows who

Sean Jackson is."

"He's nice. Super sweet with Jasmine. So this book…"

"You're liking it?"

I grin. "*Loving* it. Owen's such a bizarre character, but I love his certainty about everything. He just *knows*."

"Knows what?"

"Exactly who he is, why he's here, and what he's going to do. Just like Jasmine, actually."

"Does Jasmine talk in all caps, too?"

"No, but she *lives* in all caps. She wants to manage one of those monster resort hotels in Vegas, like the Bellagio or Caesar's Palace, one day. She's been determined to make it happen since she was a kid."

"Huh," Ben says. "I wonder what it feels like to be that confident about your future."

I sigh. "Wish I knew."

"But you have to have a pretty clear idea for yourself, too, right? Honors Chemistry at eighteen doesn't just happen. You have to have a plan."

He's not wrong; I did have a plan. I do. I always have. It's just getting harder and harder to see it lately. "Mostly my plan was to be like my dad."

"He's a scientist, too?"

"A chemist. He works for Park Pharmaceuticals. He's working on a drug now in clinical trials that increases the effectiveness of chemotherapy in cancer patients, so doctors can use less chemo and get more effective, targeted results."

"Wow."

"I know, right? He saves lives. Like, he's in a lab all day, but at the other end, people might live who would have died before. And…" I hesitate. Should I really share this with Ben?

We barely know each other— What if I'm oversharing? But he's silently waiting for me to continue, and I don't know, he seems like the kind of guy who'd be cool about it. "See, my mom died of cancer when I was ten."

"Oh, Jesus, I'm sorry."

"No, it's okay. I'm okay. My parents were always chemists with an interest in pharmaceuticals— That's how they met, in chemistry class in college. But after we lost her…Well, it's more than a job for Dad. He's stayed at Park even though he could make more money someplace else because he believes in the work they do. The drugs they're developing could help so many people. He wants to make a difference."

"And so do you?"

"Yeah. I do."

"So you're going to be a chemist, too. That's cool."

I grimace. "But…"

A pause. "But what?"

I hesitate. "I failed my first chem test. Like, I *bombed* it. I've been doing chemistry experiments with my dad since I was four. Projects, science fair entries, special assignments— We've done it all together."

"That's great," Ben says. "You're lucky to have that kind of relationship with him."

"But that's the thing— The minute I was on my own, I crashed and burned."

"It's your first semester. It's rough for everybody. You'll get a handle on it soon."

"Maybe I don't want to."

The words just hang there, and I can't take them back. I can't believe I even said them. To *Ben*, of all people, who I barely know. I bite my lip and close my eyes, fighting a lump in my chest that aches with every breath.

"Are you having some sort of existential crisis while reading *Owen Meany*, Hannah?" Ben asks with a laugh. Thank God he laughs. If he didn't laugh, I'd probably start crying.

"Maybe. Bet you never expected that when you gave it to me."

"Books can be dangerous. You never know when they're going to blow up, and what they'll take out when they do. Why do you think dictators are so fond of burning them? One idea can lead to another, and then before you know it, people are going crazy having thoughts and opinions and stuff."

Now *I'm* laughing. Actually laughing, even though I just said something that kind of throws my whole life into chaos. But Ben said the exact right thing, and for a moment, I can breathe.

"So what are you going to do now? Change majors?"

Moment over. My heart races, and my throat goes tight. Change majors? No—I couldn't—could I? I shake my head. "No way. I worked too hard to get here. And the whole thing with my mom… My dad would be devastated."

Ben sighs. "I know something about disappointed fathers."

He sounds so sad and tired. I frown. "That sounds serious."

"Nah." He huffs dismissively. "I've just never really been the son he wanted me to be."

And yet, in the bookstore last weekend, when Ben talked about not having enough time to read everything he wanted to, he was so passionate. He loves being there, working there, talking about books. How could a parent be disappointed in someone who's found their calling?

"What makes you think that?" I ask.

"Pretty sure he's asked me if I'm gay half a dozen times."

My chest seizes up. That never even crossed my mind. If Ben is gay... I clear my throat and try to sound casual. "Are you?"

"Not at all. I'm just so different from my dad that the only explanation he can come up with is that I'm gay."

Oh, thank God. I exhale slowly. "What makes you guys so different?"

"It would be faster to list what doesn't. He's a wealth manager. Do you know what that is?"

"Not really."

Ben chuckles. "Neither do I. But he's *really* good at it. He tells me all about it, but it's like he's speaking another language. Which is fine— I don't need to understand his job. But it's everything else, too. He's into high-end electronics and sports cars; I'm into old books. He likes football; I like baseball. The list goes on. My parents probably wonder if they brought the wrong kid home from the hospital."

"Just because you're different people, that doesn't mean he's not proud of you."

"Can you really be proud of someone when you think what they're doing with their life is pointless?"

I wince. "Your dad said that?"

"Once or twice."

"I'm sorry."

"It's no big deal. At least he's got my brother, who's like his clone, so he got *one* perfect son."

"You have a brother?"

"Gavin. He's two years older than me. Just started a training program with some investment firm in Chicago that

Dad set up for him."

He sounds so isolated, his father and brother so similar and Ben on the outside. "I'm sorry. That sounds really lonely."

Ben laughs. "I didn't mean to sound melodramatic. I'm fine, really. How did we get here anyway? Weren't we talking about *A Prayer for Owen Meany*?"

"Yeah. This was fun, though." I press my palm against my heated cheek and smile. Thank God he can't see me right now.

"Yeah, it was. So are you coming in this weekend for a new book?"

"Absolutely."

"I guess I better start thinking about it then. 'Night, Hannah."

"Good night, Ben."

Chapter Six

" S o was The Cemetery of Forgotten Books really a magical place or was that just how Daniel perceived it? Or I guess how the reader perceived it?"

I'm sitting on the stool that Ben hauled out from some dusty backroom and set next to the counter. He's working his way through a huge stack of used books, looking them up online, determining their value, and pricing them. The blue glow of the computer reflects in his glasses, obscuring his eyes. Just like the first time I saw him.

We've been talking about the book I read last week, *The Shadow of the Wind,* while he works. Except all this talk about books he loves was too much temptation for Ben, so this week, he reread *The Shadow of the Wind* with me, which has been fun in a whole new way. The book is magical and romantic, and of the books he's chosen for me, this is the first love story. Does that mean something? I want it to.

And yet, watching Ben as he painstakingly prices books, it wouldn't seem so. He's had ample opportunity to take this beyond friendship, and I've made myself available. We text all through the day and talk on the phone almost every night, but it hasn't gone any further. Jasmine says give it time, but I'm impatient.

"That's the great thing about books," Ben says. "As opposed to movies or, God forbid, real life— The only thing that matters is how the reader perceives it."

Prometheus Books is chilly most of the time, but today the ancient radiators have kicked on with a vengeance, and it's really warm inside. Ben has shed his usual hoodie, and he's in just a gray T-shirt. He's as lean as I suspected, and all spare, smooth muscles and elegantly angled bones. Nothing about Ben is wasted space, and I can't take my eyes off him.

I admire his forearms as he types. "What do you mean?"

"Well, the writer writes it, and while that's happening, the writer is the god of that universe. But then the book goes out into the world, and it belongs to the readers. Whatever the writer intended, there's only what the reader perceives." Ben swivels on his stool to face me, and the shock of his fiery, dark eyes makes my heart skip a beat. "Every reader perceives it differently because we all bring our own experiences and our own realities to the table. Doesn't that blow your mind?"

Whoa. I'd never really thought of reading that way.

Ben pushes his glasses up his nose and pivots back to the computer. "Maybe that's just me."

"No, I get it. I do." I touch his arm. His skin is warm and smooth, and you'd think he'd be pale from being inside all the time, but he's not. His arms have just a hint of gold. I could stare at them for the rest of my life. *Focus, Hannah.* "And that's really cool," I finally force out. "My experience reading this book is different from yours."

Ben smiles at me over his shoulder, and my knees go weak. "Exactly."

God, he's gorgeous.

"So you didn't answer my question: the Cemetery of Forgotten Books. Real or imagined? He wrote about it like it was real, but how could a place like that really exist?"

"I totally answered your question."

"You did not."

He sighs dramatically. "For me, the Cemetery of Forgotten Books is painfully, excruciatingly real, because I so desperately want it to be a real place. A repository filled with used books so that they're never forgotten— Can you imagine? But maybe for you it's a metaphor. Maybe the narrator was young and impressionable, and it was just a room with a lot of old books in it. In the world of the novel, both can be true."

"Ohhhh. Okay."

"So… What do you think? Real or not real?"

"What kind of question is that?"

"I want to know if you believe in magic, Hannah. Or is science the master of us all?"

I'm staring at him, his wide, lopsided smile, smooth skin, and hair in revolt, and yes, I *so* believe in magic, because only magic can explain the way he makes me feel.

I smile and shake my head, which isn't much of an answer. He chuckles and turns back to his computer screen. I run my fingertip along the edge of my book. The dust jacket is torn along the spine and taped back together. Inside the front cover, someone has written an inscription.

To Margaret, In fond remembrance of Stuttgart. Love, Michael.

What happened in Stuttgart? Why was this book for sale in a used bookstore? Why did Margaret, whoever she is, give it away? One of the great things about used books is they carry their own stories beyond the ones told in the pages.

"Ben, do you want to take a break?" Adele says. She materializes at odd times and with no warning.

Ben looks amused and puzzled, too. "Um, sure. I suppose I could use a break. Hannah, want to get a drink with me?"

Like I'm going to say no to that. Or anything else he suggests. "Sure."

I follow him out of the store to a coffee place across the street from Prometheus. He perks up as soon as we get inside. Maybe Adele was right about him needing a break.

"It was more than just the Cemetery of Lost Books that seemed magical," I say, continuing our conversation from the store. He looks at me and blinks in confusion.

"The Shadow of the Wind. The whole thing felt a little magical, don't you think? Spain, the town they lived in, the way he wrote it, it all felt a bit like a dark fairy tale."

"Oh, right." He nods and looks toward the front of the line again. "His writing is very lyrical. Evocative."

"It makes me want to go there. Have you ever been?"

"Where?"

"Spain."

He shakes his head. "France on a school trip in high school, but that's all. You?"

"I haven't been anywhere."

We're up next, and the counter girl smiles broadly at Ben. "Hey, Ben! Taking a break?"

He shrugs and smiles back. "I need a pick-me-up."

I bet he knows everybody in these shops along Clark Street. It's nice, like a little neighborhood.

The barista smiles at me, too. She's pretty, tall, with long, dark hair, high cheekbones, and blue eyes so pale they look like ice. There's something smart and sophisticated about her. She looks out of place behind the register in a coffee shop, like she should be in a boardroom instead.

Ben motions to me. "This is Hannah."

"Hey, I'm Alex. What can I get for you guys today?"

Her smile is infectious. I like her, even though her beauty is a little intimidating. "Hot chocolate," I say. "My favorite."

"That sounds good. Me, too." He looks at Alex. "You know, for a change."

Alex smiles at us. "Okay, two hot chocolates. Gimme a sec."

When she turns away to make our order, Ben and I shift down the counter and out of the way.

"You must come here all the time, huh?"

He glances across the counter. "Yeah, it's close and I'm friends with most of the people that work here. Alex comes into the store a lot."

She does? Everything suddenly feels awkward— Is he friends with everyone or mostly Alex? "She seems nice."

"She is."

Alex comes back a minute later with our drinks and rings us up. "Careful," she cautions. "They're really hot."

"You working all day today?" he asks her.

"Closing tonight." She rolls her eyes. "On a Saturday. No

worse fate."

"Do you have plans after?"

I frown. It almost sounds like they're more than see-each-other-at-work friends. Is there something going on between them?

"Dinner with friends. I'll get there late, but it's better than nothing."

Ben nods. "Sounds fun. Well, I'd better get back. See you around."

"See you. Nice to meet you, Hannah. See you around, too, I guess?"

She's smiling like my hanging around with Ben is the best thing ever, so maybe I'm off base. Maybe they really are just friends. "Sure."

Back at Prometheus, we talk a little more about *The Shadow of the Wind* while Ben takes forever picking out another book for me. He convinces himself three times and changes his mind three times. Finally, he settles on one and passes it to me. I reach for my wallet, but he stops me.

"Forget it. It's a loan. I know you'll be back with it."

"I will. For sure. Are there any big moments when I should text you in this one?"

"Nah, we'll just talk about it as you go."

I love his casual mention of our frequent phone calls, his assumption that they'll continue. A few customers have come in while we were talking. Adele is handling one, but another lady is wandering around, and even I can tell she can't find what she's looking for.

I should clear out and let Ben do his job. But we've had such a great afternoon, and this feels like it's growing into something more. He hasn't made a move, but maybe I need to drop a hint? God, I wish Jasmine was here. She's so much better at this.

"What are you up to tonight?"

Ben shrugs. "Hanging out with John at home, I guess."

I pause— I left the opportunity open for him, is he going to take it?

Ask me what I'm up to. Ask me to hang out with you.

But he doesn't. Instead, he shuffles a stack of books out of the way of the register and adjusts his glasses, smiling at me awkwardly. I fight the swell of disappointment prickling my eyes and making my stomach feel heavy as I slip my new book into my bag.

"Maybe I'll call you if I start this tonight," I say.

"Yeah, you should. That'd be great."

I hesitate for another second, just in case, but no. He's not going to ask. "Okay, talk to you soon."

"Yep. See you, Hannah." He waves, then turns away. "Ma'am? If you're looking for something specific, I might be able to help you find it."

That's my cue, and I ignore my sinking stomach as I head home. I should probably study for chem. I have another test coming up soon, a chance to redeem myself a little bit. But I probably won't. I think I'm starting a new book instead.

Chapter Seven

"Ben, can I talk to you for a minute?" Professor Donnelly asks as I pack up my stuff after Thursday's class.

"Sure. What's up?"

Donnelly nods good-bye to a student, then turns back to me. "That was good work you did on the Osborne this week. Very reasoned arguments and well supported by the text."

"Thank you, sir."

"Have you given any more thought to your plans for next year?"

My stomach twists, and I rub the back of my neck. "A bit."

Professor Donnelly smiles. "Is grad school a possibility for you?"

"Um… I have a lot to consider." Like law school.

"I'd like you to consider pursuing your MA. You're the

best student I've had in many years, and I think our graduate program would be a great fit for you."

Holy shit. I told Hannah about this weeks ago, but in that things-you-want-that-never-happen-in-real-life kind of way. But here's Donnelly, the head of the department and the professor I admire the most, telling me he wants me to stay on. I can't believe it. "Thank you, sir."

"The deadline for the application is coming up soon, so don't wait too long."

"I won't." I hadn't even seriously considered applying, but now? The idea is unfurling in my brain, so alluring and perfect. Could I really do this? Could I get into the grad program, get my master's, and keep studying what I *want* to study?

"See you next week, Ben." He slips the rest of his papers into his battered leather bag and leaves.

Fuck.

Working on my master's under Donnelly would be a dream come true. But the reality is there's no way my parents will go along with grad school when they're so against my major. It's law school or nothing.

I haven't crunched the numbers on what a master's program at Arlington State runs, never mind a PhD, but I'm guessing it far exceeds my shitty bank account. I spend all my waking hours at Prometheus because I love it there, not because Ralph is lining my pockets with a fat salary.

Of course, there's my trust fund, which isn't a ton of money, but it'd be enough. But I don't get access to that until I'm twenty-five, which does me no good right now.

A couple hours later, I'm squinting at the computer screen and working my way through pricing a stack of books at Prometheus, and I'm still no closer to any kind of insight.

Last time I saw my dad, he gave me some crap about how living out your dreams is kid stuff. Adults choose a sensible path and stick to it. He's probably right, but hell, that dream is so damn appealing. I can't shut it down, no matter how much I try.

The bell rings as the door opens, and Hannah sweeps in, bringing a gust of cool, crisp fall air in her wake. Something thrums inside me as she meets my eyes. The breeze has turned her cheeks and lips pink. Her eyes sparkle like she's about to burst with her latest literary revelation. I can almost hear every dusty, aged page in the store ruffle slightly with her arrival. It feels like I do, too.

I smile. "Hey."

She plants her palms onto the counter and leans toward me. "You have to tell me Joe comes back."

"What?"

"Joe. He just found out his brother died and he left. He comes back, right? He's not *gone* gone."

I'm still so distracted by her wind-bitten lips that it takes me a second to remember what she's reading right now, but it comes back to me: *The Amazing Adventures of Kavalier and Clay.*

"Ben!" Her eyes widen.

She's so cute when she gets caught up in the story. "Guess you'll have to keep reading and see," I tease.

"But what about Rosa?"

I shrug. "What about her?"

"He just *left* her."

"His brother died."

"But he loves her. Tell me he's coming right back."

"Keep reading, Hannah."

"Ughhh. You're no help." She circles around the counter and flops down onto the stool that I leave for her visits. Her backpack slides down her arm and hits the ground with a thud. Her despair is almost comical.

I chuckle. "Where's the fun if I just tell you what's going to happen?"

"Okay, fine. Don't tell me. Now I'm going to be up all night reading."

"Call me and I'll keep you company, even if you're tucked up in bed." *Whoa, hold up.* Where did that come from? But Hannah just smiles— Maybe it didn't throw her?

"You know I will. If I'm awake, so are you." Then her gaze drops to my chest and she laughs. "What the hell happened to your shirt?"

"What?" I glance down—oh, right. I ran out of decent clothes this week. This is my pink splotchy shirt. "Ah… I had an incident in the laundry room. Some of my white clothes look like this now."

"Did you seriously not separate the red clothes?"

"I always forget. I'm terrible at this stuff. Anyway, you've been in college for what, two months? It's not like you have loads of laundry experience yourself."

"I've been doing laundry since I was ten."

My face goes hot. Shit. Her mom. I forgot. "I'm so sorry. I forgot about your mom."

"It's okay. I'm pretty sure I'd have been doing laundry even with both parents around. Your parents never made you do laundry at home?"

I shrug. "We had a maid."

Hannah sputters out a disbelieving laugh. "Seriously?"

"Yeah."

"I've never known anyone who had a maid before. I guess that investment stuff your dad does pays pretty well."

I grimace. "It did for him."

"Lucky you. So how's your day going, rich boy?"

"I'm not rich." Then again, I *do* have that trust fund. In Hannah's eyes, that probably makes me rich, even though I don't have any control over it. "My day is fine, I guess. Just…"

Her eyebrows furrow and she straightens up. "Is something wrong?"

"No, not wrong. I don't know yet." I push my glasses back up my nose. "One of my professors wants me to apply to the master's program."

"Wow, that's great!" She touches my arm, and I feel it in my stomach. My gaze flies to hers, but she's smiling, hand still on my forearm, oblivious. Did she feel it, too? Her face is so calm; it's hard to say. "I mean, that's great, right?" she presses.

"I…don't know."

Hannah laughs and runs her hand down to my wrist, squeezing gently. My pulse races, and the room goes hot. Does she realize what she's doing? She must. I should pull away, but… It feels kind of nice.

"Ben, it's like you were made for this." She smiles. "What is there to decide?"

This is so easy for her, a freshman with years ahead of her to figure it all out. I stare out the storefront, watching pedestrians walk past, enjoying the weather.

"I don't know." I sigh. "I'm supposed to go to law school. Actually, my dad really wants me to work in finance like him and my brother, but he gave up on that dream ages ago. Law school is an acceptable second choice, though."

She bursts out laughing. My stomach sinks. Yeah, I don't think I'm a natural for law school, either, but nobody's ever *laughed* at the idea of it before.

"I'm sorry, *law school*?" She struggles to catch her breath. "*You?*"

"You think I can't do it?"

"Ben, you're brilliant. I know you *can* do it. I don't think you *want* to do it."

And that makes Hannah the only person to figure it out. My family certainly never cared that my heart isn't in it, and whenever I talk about law school with Alex, she just gets excited and starts chattering non-stop about all the programs I should look into. Still, as right as Hannah is, people don't always get what they want. I sure don't.

"My dad's got a point, though. Maybe it's stupid to spend all these years in college just reading books and shit." I shove the pile I'm currently working on off to the side. Books. My whole damn life is about books, and for what? "Maybe I should think about what I'm going to do with the rest of my life. At least law pays well."

"Who cares about money?" she asks quietly. "You'd be an amazing teacher, Ben. I know you would."

"Yeah, but I'm not sure—"

"This is just like Sam."

I frown. "Who?"

"Sammy Clay, in the book."

Oh. She's talking about *Kavalier and Clay*. "In what way?"

"Him and Tracy," she says, referencing Sam's closeted relationship with Tracy, the Hollywood actor. Seriously?

"I told you I'm not gay."

She laughs again. "I know. I meant the way Sam is denying himself and who he really is. How long do you think he can manage that? I haven't finished the book yet, but you have, and I'm betting that part of the story doesn't work out well."

No, it doesn't. It doesn't work out well for Sam or anybody around him. "It's complicated." That's kind of a cop-out, but I can't figure this out today. "And what about you, anyway?"

"Me?"

I give her a pointed look. "You've been having mixed feelings about your major, too. What are you going to do about it?"

Hannah looks away, fidgeting with the zipper on her jacket. "I've been working on it. I'm sure I'll do much better on the next test. It was just first semester jitters, like you said."

"Sounded like more than that to me."

"I told you, this is about so much more than a major. It's about my mom, too."

"I know, but Hannah, you can't do something you hate just for her sake. You know that, right?"

"It's—"

"Complicated. Yeah, I know."

She sighs and rolls her eyes. "Look, let's forget all this stuff. I just came by to see if you wanted to go get some hot chocolate with me. Want to?"

Alex isn't working today—I already checked—but... "Yeah, sure. Why not?" I turn toward the shelves. "Hey, Adele? I'm going out for a minute."

"Okay," her voice answers faintly from the back. "Hi, Hannah!"

"Hi, Adele!" she calls back.

We head out and cross the street to Coffee Oasis.

"This weather…" Hannah closes her eyes and tips her face to the sky. Her light brown hair, eyebrows, and eyelashes explode with gold when the sun hits them. She's almost glittering; it's startling, the way it transforms her. She's beautiful. "I'm going to miss it when the snow starts."

I clear my throat and force myself to look away. "Me, too."

Alex isn't working, but Marc is, and I know him a little. Oasis is quiet, so he chats us up as he makes our hot chocolates.

"So what are you guys up to today?"

"Oh, I'm working at Prometheus. Hannah just stopped in to visit."

"You go to Arlington State, Hannah?"

"Yeah, this is my first year. You?"

"Now and then." Marc smirks. He's been a part-time student for nearly a decade—if you can call auditing one class a year part-time. The rest of the time he scrapes by working at the Oasis and selling weed. The girls seem to find him charming. I don't get it. "Whipped cream on these?"

"Umm…" Hannah hesitates. "I'm not sure."

Marc grins at her over his shoulder. "Oh, come on. Indulge a little." I scowl at him— He's looking at her like *she's* the whipped cream. What an asshole.

But I need to relax. Hannah isn't my girlfriend, and this isn't a date.

She laughs and nods. "Okay, sure. Whipped cream."

"Thatta girl." He piles it on thick, like his bullshit. I'm glaring at his back, but the fucker is oblivious. I mean, come on, Hannah's cute, but she's also way too young and sweet for a washed-up burnout like Marc.

"Okay, two hot chocolates. Six fifty."

"I got this." I pull out my wallet without thinking. It feels like one-upping Marc, somehow, but I doubt anyone notices.

"Thanks." Hannah sips hers and looks at me over the rim of the cup. Her eyelashes are so long they cast little feathery shadows across the tops of her cheekbones. I take a long sip of my hot chocolate before I say something inexplicably stupid.

Mistake. It's piping hot and burns my tongue. While I'm breathing in and out, trying to cool the burn, Hannah chuckles.

"You have whipped cream on your lip."

I swipe at my upper lip, the obvious culprit, but she shakes her head.

"No, here." She reaches out and slides her thumb against the corner of my mouth. Her finger is soft and warm on my lips, then on my cheek as she drags her hand away. My skin tingles long after she stops touching me.

"Got it," she murmurs, and then she slips her thumb, slicked with whipped cream, into her mouth. Something flips over in my stomach as her pink lips curve around her finger. I've just wandered into someplace dangerous.

"I should get back to the store."

"Oh. Sure," Hannah says. "I have class in half an hour. I better get going. I'll call you later, once I know if Joe comes back."

"Joe?"

Hannah rolls her eyes. "The book, silly."

Right. The book. I almost forgot.

Chapter Eight

HANNAH

"Adele, this book— It just *killed* me."

"I knew it would." Adele laughs. "In a good way."

I clutch my chest. "Good, yes. But I don't think I'll ever be the same."

"A good book will do that to you."

Last week, after I finished *The Amazing Adventures of Kavalier and Clay*, Adele got frustrated when Ben took too long to decide on the next book I should read. So she shoved *The Poisonwood Bible* into my hands and sent me out the door.

She was so right. Talk about a shift in perspective. Even better, Ben had never read it, so we went through it together this week and talked for ages on the phone every night. He loved the book, but I don't think he was moved the way I was. Maybe he's just seen more of the world than I have.

"So, Africa," I say to Adele. "I feel like I could spend the rest of my life just reading about Africa."

"There are other books," Ben protests from behind the counter. "I have some ideas about your next read."

"Of course you do, sweetie." Adele pats his hand consolingly. "But Hannah's got to get her feelings out about this one first."

Ben frowns and Adele laughs.

"Let the girl like her book, Ben." That girl, Alex, from the coffee shop across the street is spending her break in the store. She's leaning on the counter, flipping through a magazine, and occasionally contributing to the conversation happening around her.

Ben frowns but he doesn't say anything.

"There is no place on earth like Africa," Adele says. "I was there, you know."

"You were?"

She nods, and her eyes fill with tears. "In seventy-one, with the Peace Corps. We were in Zambia, not the Congo, like they were in the book. But the people... Oh, they laughed at us at first. And we did plenty to earn that laughter. But once they understood we really wanted to help, and once we understood there are lots of ways to help outside of training stipulations, they treated us like family. We did a lot of good. It broke my heart to leave. I felt like I was leaving part of myself behind."

"Why don't you go back?" I ask.

"I loved it, but it wasn't easy. And I'm too old now. That's a young person's life. That's an adventure for someone like you."

I blink. "Me? Oh, no, I could never do something like that."

Adele draws herself up and fixes me with her steady stare. "Why not? I wasn't much older than you when I went."

"I just never—I'm not..." How do I explain I'm not that girl? I'm the girl who can carefully monitor chemical compounds in a sterile lab, or track complex data across multiple spreadsheets. I'm not the girl who hikes into the African wilderness, joins a village, and changes the world.

Unless... Maybe I could be? I'd never even thought about it. I mean, I should have been amazing at chemistry, so who knows? Maybe the reverse is true, too. I might be great at things I should suck at.

"You can do anything you set your mind to, Hannah," Adele says. "Here, give this one a try next."

She passes me a book also set in Africa called *Things Fall Apart*.

"Thanks, Adele."

"But I already picked out your book for this week," Ben protests.

"Hold that thought, Ben." Adele smiles and hands me yet another book. "And if you want to see a little more about Africa, take a look at this book about the Bang Bang Club."

"The what club?"

"It was a group of photojournalists working in South Africa during Apartheid."

"Ooh, I saw a movie about them," Alex chimes in. "Lots of cute guys."

There aren't any cute guys in this book, but I spend twenty minutes lost in it just the same. It's another world, like nothing I've ever experienced. All I know of the world outside of Ohio is what I see on the nightly news, and it's no-where near enough. There are people and worlds out there I've never even glimpsed.

But I want to be a chemist, like my dad. I want to work in a lab, creating medicines that save lives, like my mom's. That's making a difference. That's changing the world. And yet, looking at these photographs of Africa in the nineties... Maybe there are a million ways to make a difference and a million differences that need to be made.

Could I make a difference outside of a lab? It's a ques-tion I've never asked myself.

"These are amazing," I murmur. "Chilling, but amazing."

"If you like photojournalism, you should look at this one, too." Adele deposits another book in my lap.

I didn't know I was into photojournalism, but before I know it, I'm caught up in it. Civil wars in Bosnia, famine in Africa, floods in New Orleans, oppression in North Korea — The litany of human suffering and need goes on and on. Formulating drugs in a laboratory might be a noble calling, but what if it's not my calling? What would that mean for me? For my dad?

"Have I lost you to Adele's social causes forever?" Ben stands next to us with a wry smile, hands shoved in his back pockets.

"No, it's just...these pictures."

"Let her expand her mind if she wants to," Adele says.

"She's been reading my books for weeks. I think that's pretty mind-expanding."

I touch Ben's arm to get his attention. "I'm not throwing over reading. I just got caught up in these pictures. I can't stop thinking about them. And I can't stop thinking about

The Poisonwood Bible. And *The Book Thief.* And Owen. And Joe and Sam. What have you done to me?"

Ben smiles, and my heart thuds helplessly in my chest. "Whatever it is, I hope it's just the start. So I know Adele just gave you a book, but how would you feel about reading something just because it's funny?"

"That sounds great. What do you have in mind?"

"Something really good, but you have to read this one with me."

"We read all of them together. I call you almost every night."

"Oh, no, I think this requires pizza and reading out loud," he says with a chuckle. "You busy tonight?"

Something flutters in my stomach, and my pulse races. I think I might have just died and gone to heaven because unless I'm totally misreading this, Ben wants to hang out tonight. Together. Like a date. This is a date, right? I have to fight to keep my smile to normal human levels. "I guess I'm busy now."

"Hey, Alex, you want to come?" he asks, and something inside me curls up and dies. I'd forgotten Alex was here, but Ben didn't. Why is he inviting her? Is this *not* a date? She glances up, surprised, and shakes her head.

"Oh, no thanks. I have a thing. You guys go and have fun. Sounds like Ben has something good picked out, Hannah."

And she's so damn nice about it that I can't even be annoyed. She's all but winking at me, telling me to go for it. And if I were a little bit braver, I just might.

W e're in my dorm room, we split a pizza an hour ago, and I'm lying back on my bed, propped up by pillows. Ben was lying across the foot of my bed, head and shoulders against the concrete block wall, but now he's pacing the tiny open space between my bed and Jasmine's, reading out loud from *A Confederacy of Dunces*.

"What *is* this book, Ben?" I'm laughing so hard that my sides hurt and I can barely breathe. Ben's laughing, too, but desperately trying to get it under control so he can keep reading.

"This is *A Confederacy of Dunces*. Show some respect. It won a fucking Pulitzer Prize."

The best part—the very best part—of reading this book together is that Ben keeps snatching it out of my hands so he can read his favorite parts out loud to me. And he doesn't just read; he *acts them out*, with a crazy voice for Ignatius and everything. I'm dying. It's the most I've laughed in forever.

"Come on, Hannah," he scolds. "Pull it together. *God.*" He gives an exaggerated eye roll and holds the book up with a flourish. "Listen to this. 'I am, at the moment, writing a lengthy indictment against our century. When my brain begins to reel from my literary labors, I make an occasional cheese dip.' Can't you just *feel* Ignatius's soul cry out?"

I double over laughing, and finally Ben gives in, too, falling across my bed and laughing until his eyes tear up. Gasping for air, I pull myself upright and reach for the book, but my hand lands on his hand instead. My fingers curl loosely around his wrist, and I trace the sculptural bones just like I've imagined so many times. He's still lying across my bed, just shy of my feet. He's so close. I could lean down and—

Our eyes meet, and my whole body flushes with awareness. The air around us is charged, like if we kiss, it'll spark.

I want to find out. His eyes are wide behind his glasses, wary and surprised. And maybe something else. I can't be the only one feeling this.

Then, quick as a flash, his gaze drops to my mouth and back up to my eyes. I'm not the only one feeling whatever this is. I can't be. I'm not sure I'm brave enough to make a move, but he could so easily. All he has to do is lean forward. I'll even meet him halfway. I start leaning slightly, just a hint for him to take—

Jasmine blows into our room with Sean in tow. Sean is enormous, and our tiny dorm room looks like a doll's house with him standing in the middle of it.

"Oh!" she gasps, her eyes flickering between Ben and me. "I didn't know you were home. Or had a guest."

Ben scrambles off my bed so fast you'd think it was on fire. "That's okay. I was just about to go." He glances at me, not quite meeting my eyes. "I have to open the store in the morning, so…"

"Oh, sure. Um. This is Jasmine, my roommate, and her boyfriend, Sean. This is Ben."

Jasmine extends her hand and puts on her CEO smile. "Nice to meet you, Ben."

He shakes her hand, and then he and Sean exchange an awkward handshake, too. "Nice to meet you guys. Okay, I'm gonna head out. Enjoy the rest of the book, Hannah." Now he does meet my eyes, just for a second, and he smiles slightly. Then he slips out the door like he was never here.

"So," Jasmine says when the door closes behind him. "Bookstore Boy is *cute*."

"Excuse me?" Sean says.

Jasmine pats his shoulder. "Relax. Bookstore Boy is Hannah's. I'm just making an observation."

I sigh and flop back on my bed. "Bookstore Boy is most *definitely* not mine. Did you see how fast he cut out of here? God, that was embarrassing."

"Maybe because we interrupted him when he was about to make his move. Looked pretty cozy in here when we opened the door."

I glance at Sean, blushing that he's here to witness my humiliation, but his eyes are fixed firmly on the floor. He looks like he'd rather be anywhere else on earth than here listening to this.

"Yeah, except he had all night to kiss me." And he almost did. Didn't he? What would've happened if we'd had a few extra seconds?

Jasmine chews on her fingernail and frowns. "He was in this room with you all night—alone—and he didn't kiss you once? And you're sure he's not gay?"

"Definitely not. He's established that twice."

"And there's no girlfriend?"

My stomach churns. A girlfriend? No, I would've known…right? "He hasn't specifically said so, but I think at this point it would have come up. I'm at the shop enough that I'd have met her or heard about her, right?"

Unless I *do* know about her. Alex is gorgeous, older than me, and she's known Ben a lot longer. But I'd have noticed if they were together, wouldn't I? And today after Ben invited her to come along with us, she said no and gave me an encouraging smile. That's girl code. She was practically telling me to go for it— She wouldn't have done that if they were dating.

"Guys can hide that shit if they want to, but since he's not moving in on you, I can't imagine why he'd hide something," Jasmine says. "That's usually reserved for the cheating scumbags."

I flop back onto my bed, clutching *A Confederacy of Dunces* to my chest. The rest of the book is probably going to pale in comparison to the parts we read together. "Maybe I'm just wrong about all of this. Maybe he's not into me like that."

"A guy doesn't end up alone in a girl's dorm room on a Friday night, lying on her bed, if he's not into her at least a little bit," Sean interrupts.

Jasmine and I stare at him, and he shrugs one massive shoulder. "I'm just saying this was a situation. You don't get there by accident. He had to want to on some level."

Sean's right. Ben's eyes were wary as we looked at each other, but there was also interest. And the way he looked at my mouth… For a split second, he was thinking about it. "So why did he bolt out of here?"

Sean holds up his hands. "Who knows? Maybe the dude's got some hang-ups or something."

I groan and close my eyes. "Well, whatever it is, I'm pretty sure it means I'm out of luck."

Jasmine sits on the edge of my bed. "You going to be okay? We just stopped by so I could grab my calculus book, but I can stay if you want me to."

"No, that's really nice of you, but I'm fine."

Jasmine smiles and squeezes my knee. "Maybe you need to take control of this and make the first move," she says. "Just putting it out there. Think about it."

I wave them both out the door. I should forget about it at least for tonight, but when I lie on my bed and stare at the ceiling, I can't help it— Ben's stare haunts me for the rest of the night.

Chapter Nine

BEN

It's been a week since the incident in Hannah's dorm, and I still can't get her face out of my mind. Truth is, I don't even know *what* that was. I sort of guessed Hannah was into me, and yeah, she's cute. Really cute. But that night last week when she leaned toward me, she wasn't cute anymore— She was soft lips and fluttering eyelashes, and fuck, I wanted to kiss her. I wanted to kiss her, press her back onto the bed, and do a whole lot more than kissing.

I freaked out, and I've spent all week figuring out what to do. But now I know. I just lost my focus; that's all. Alex. Alex is the one I want. That's the plan. It was always the plan.

Today is the day I refocus. It's Alex's birthday, and I've bought her a necklace—a delicate gold heart with a tiny diamond set in it. Definitely not a gift for a girl who's just a friend. Giving her the necklace will make my intentions unmistakable.

"Ben?" Adele calls as she makes her way up the aisle. "I can't find that copy of *The Aeneid* for the phone order that came in. Is it still in the computer?"

I tap a few keys as Adele leans onto the counter. "Inventory says it's here. But there's this other copy of *The Aeneid* that Elliot supposedly sold last week. I bet he clicked on the wrong copy. Idiot."

"Can you email that nice lady back and tell her we don't have it anymore?"

"Sure, I'll take care of it."

Her gaze falls on Alex's present wrapped and ready to go on the counter, and she arches an eyebrow. "Oooh, what have you got here?"

"It's for Alex. Today is her birthday."

Adele tips her head to the side. It's impossible to miss, based on the size and shape, that it's a jewelry box. "I see." She sighs, sounding disappointed. "Well, I'm sure she'll love it."

Adele drifts away, and I stare at her back. I haven't missed that she's been playing matchmaker with Hannah and me, but she should know better. I've felt this way about Alex since way before Hannah ever showed up. Maybe I was slow to make it happen, but today I'm going to fix that.

As soon as the clock hits two, which is when Alex's shift starts today, I grab the present and head out to Coffee Oasis. I glance through the plate glass front window— Alex is tying her apron around her waist and laughing at something. When she laughs, she throws her head back and her whole body lights up; she's absolutely gorgeous.

One deep breath and I push through the door. It's mid-afternoon, so thankfully there aren't a lot of customers. Marc is dealing with two girls at the counter while Alex refills a napkin dispenser.

"Hey."

She looks up and smiles. "Hey, Ben."

With no preamble, I pass the gift across the counter to her. "Happy birthday."

Her smile fades as she takes it. "Wow. Did you—"

"Today's your birthday, right?"

"Yeah, it is. I just... I can't believe you got me something."

"Of course I did." I force a smile even though my body is thrumming with nerves. "Go ahead and open it."

My stomach is in knots as she tears the paper off. She flips the top of the box, and her eyes go wide.

"Oh, wow, Ben... It's way too much."

"No such thing as too much for your birthday."

She sighs and smiles at me. "That's really sweet, Ben."

My heart sinks. *Sweet?* Sweet is a guy saving a seat for you, or loaning you his lecture notes. How about "you know me so well" or "this is perfect and I love it." She's acting like I bought her a coffee or something. I swallow down my disappointment and push ahead with my plan.

"So, do you have any great plans for your birthday?" *Because if you don't, I'm giving you plans.*

She smirks. "You mean besides making cappuccinos for other people all afternoon?"

"After that."

"Actually, yeah. A friend of mine is having a party."

I deflate inside. "Oh. They're throwing you a party? That's great."

"No, it's not *for* me. It's a giant house party. Like a 'it's nearly Thanksgiving break so let's all get wasted' kind of thing. Hey, you should come."

My breath catches— She's inviting me? Maybe all isn't lost, after all. "Really? You want me to come?"

"Sure. Hang on, I have the flyer somewhere." She retrieves her huge bag from under the counter and digs through it endlessly, depositing two textbooks, her laptop, makeup, hair things, and all manner of stuff onto the counter. Finally, she produces a rumpled photocopy. "Got it! I knew it was in there. I never throw anything away."

"Clearly," I joke.

She shovels all the junk back into her bag without a single chuckle and thrusts the flyer at me. "Seriously, you should come. I bet you'll have a great time."

I hold back a long sigh. I don't want to read too much into her not laughing at my joke, but shouldn't there be *some* sort of spark here? Am I being that dumb guy who can't read a girl's signals?

She did give me this flyer, though. I look at it, all bold letters and exclamation points. It's not the kind of party I'd ever go to on my own, but if she wants me there… "I'll be there."

"Great! So, you want a coffee? Birthday girl is treating."

I'd rather have hot chocolate, but it's not a big deal. I wave the flyer with a smile. "Sure. Looks like this'll be a late night. I might need it."

Chapter Ten

Today is amazing. It's gotten cold, but not too bad yet. The sun is shining, there's no snow, and my brisk walk across campus to Prometheus keeps me warm enough. I feel great. Better than great. Fantastic. Because I've finally decided today is the day I quit crushing on Ben and actually do something about it.

I had a test this week, so I haven't talked to him much since he cut out of my room last Friday night. We've texted a little about *A Confederacy of Dunces*, but nothing big.

Jasmine and I have been talking it over all week, and she's convinced I need to make the first move. As she puts it, "Bookstore Boy has probably been turned down by girls all his life. He's never going to man up."

So *I'm* manning up. I'm going to get a new book, and then I'm going to ask him to hang out with me tonight, and before the night is out, I'm going to kiss him. It feels so sub-limely right that I'm not even nervous. Once we're in the moment, he'll want me as much as I want him— After all, he already did, right? We were halfway there last week. I just need to nudge him the other half.

I turn onto Clark Street just in time to see Ben cross it and disappear into Coffee Oasis. I call out his name, but he doesn't hear me. It's fine. I'll catch him there and then go back to work with him when his break is over. We can talk then.

As I approach Coffee Oasis, I can see him through the plate glass window handing a present—a small, square, present—across the counter to Alex. It looks suspiciously like a jewelry box. Then Alex peels off the paper, and my heart sinks— That's exactly what it is.

Ben gave her jewelry, and judging from the way Alex's eyes go wide when she opens the box, it's really nice, expen-sive jewelry. Not the kind of present you'd give to a friend. Now that I'm paying attention, he looks different talking to Alex— It hits me like a hammer. *This* is what Ben looks like when he's flirting, when he's into a girl. And he's never looked at me like that.

My stomach twists. I've been so stupid. There was a reason he didn't kiss me last week, and it wasn't because he's too shy to make the first move. He just wanted to be kissing Alex.

I don't know how I missed it, the way he smiles at her and how his gaze follows every move she makes. Heat flushes my face, and my eyes sting. How could he string me along like that? Maybe he didn't make a move, but we have something. Had something. Sean said he wouldn't have ended up there with me if he didn't want to be there. It wasn't all in my head— There was a moment when we almost kissed.

So what the *fuck*?

On the other side of the glass, it gets worse. Alex digs through her bag and produces a flyer before passing it across to Ben. He's smiling and nodding. It doesn't matter what I was planning tonight, because now he has plans with her.

I'm too numb to even notice he's leaving the shop until he emerges onto the sidewalk, blinking at me. "Hey, Hannah. What's up?"

"What's *up*?" I echo.

His eyes widen, and he takes half a step back, like he's been caught at something. "Is everything okay?"

I step forward, throwing my arms wide. "You tell me. What's been going on here? Because I thought I knew, but it looks like I'm really wrong."

"What do you mean?"

"You and me."

"We're friends," he says, his voice turning defensive. I was hanging on by a thread, but his words—*that* word— pushes me over the edge. I don't want to cry in front of him, but tears roll down my cheeks, and I can't hold them back.

"Friends," I scoff. "What almost happened last week in my room was *not* something friends do."

His eyes cut away. He shifts uncomfortably and rubs the back of his neck. "Look, Hannah, I'm sorry if I gave you the wrong idea, but I'm really into Alex. I have been since before I met you."

Every word lands like a punch to the gut. How am I still standing upright? "Since before you met me? That was months ago. You've had this *thing* for her, but you've been spending all your time with *me*?"

"It's complicated," he protests.

"Oh, it's complicated? It didn't seem very complicated to me, but I guess that's because you didn't tell me everything."

His face flames. "I'm sorry if you've developed feelings for me. Maybe it's just because I'm older than you and—"

"Oh, don't pull that *bullshit* on me! I'm a freshman, not some little kid."

"You're on a different planet," he says. "Let's face it. We're in really different places in our lives. What do we even have in common besides a few books we read together?"

What do we have in *common*? I thought we had everything in common. All those nights we spent talking—and not just about the books—meant so much to me. But maybe Ben was just humoring the poor girl who doesn't read. What was this to him? Some fun distraction while he mustered up the courage to go after the girl he really wanted? Every time he picked out a book for me, it felt special, personal. Maybe he was just doing his job.

In science, boys have always written me off because I look so young. I really thought Ben was different, but I guess not. I thought we'd been building something great together, but apparently, I've just been an annoying little girl tagging along after him. Well, that's done.

"Whatever. Think of me as a kid if it makes you feel like less of a coward."

His eyes light up with anger. "A coward? Where do you get that?"

"Hiding behind this friendship with me when the whole time you really wanted someone else."

"And you're so brave, huh?" he snaps. "Have you told

your dad about chemistry yet?"

I reel back. I shared all my insecurities about school with him because I thought we were friends, because I thought we might be more — not so he could throw it back in my face. But I was as wrong about that as I have been about everything else. "Have you told your dad about grad school?" I snap back.

His jaw works as he grinds his teeth together.

"Yeah, I didn't think so. You know what? Forget it. I was obviously wrong about everything."

He raises a hand half-heartedly. "Hannah—"

"Good luck, Ben." I gesture to Alex making a latte inside, oblivious to all this drama. "With everything."

Then I turn and run. He calls my name, but I don't stop. Not until I'm out of downtown, back across the bridge, across campus, and in my dorm room. Then I fall across my bed and cry until there's nothing left.

Chapter Eleven

"You're so lucky—look at these gorgeous lashes. Usually only the boys get long lashes like this." Jasmine swipes the mascara wand one more time and leans back to examine her handiwork. "Much better. Can't even tell you've been crying."

I sigh. "I'm still not sure going out tonight is the best idea."

She plants her hands onto her hips and scowls. "There's no way I'm letting you wallow in your misery over that boy all night. You're going to dress up, get out there, get yourself a drink or two, and get busy getting over him."

I swallow around the lump in my throat. "It's not that easy."

"Of course it's not. But fake it till you make it, Hannah. Pretend you're fine and eventually you will be. You'll be surprised how well that works. Now turn around so I can get started on your hair."

Obediently, I swivel in the chair, facing the mirror as Jasmine goes at my hair with a curling iron. She's right; I don't look like I've been crying all afternoon. She put some sort of cream on my eyes that made the puffiness vanish. And she's a master with makeup.

I stare at my reflection, my pale face, my high, wide-set cheekbones, and my pointed chin. Jasmine calls my face "heart-shaped," but I call it a liability. It's a girl's face, not a woman's. My lips don't help, the top one wide and fuller than the bottom. And forget about my eyes. My long lashes make me look like an innocent little girl playing a grown-up.

This afternoon, I was shaking and full of energy and so damn angry. Now I'm just exhausted. I'm nothing at all like leggy, gorgeous, going-to-law-school Alex. Maybe Ben's more into the law school thing than he let on. Knowing now how he feels about Alex, it all starts to make sense.

Alex is beautiful, smart, and driven, just like Jasmine. She and Ben are headed in the same direction in life. It's no wonder he's so into her.

I'm just…me. Doe-eyed and too young. I haven't read anything, I haven't been anywhere, and I don't know anything, especially not what I'm going to do with my life. I'm just ordinary, uninteresting, entirely insufficient Hannah.

"Hey." Jasmine tugs on a long lock of my light brown, all-natural, boring hair. "You're getting all mopey again. Cut it out."

"She's literally every single thing I'm not," I say.

"Which is fine for *her*. That doesn't mean there's a damn thing wrong with you. You're smart and beautiful and nice. Just because he doesn't want you doesn't mean you're undesirable."

"He thinks of me as a kid."

Jasmine scoffs. "Then the boy is blind, cute glasses or not, because there's nothing childish about you. Especially once I'm done with you."

"Thanks."

Jasmine has been so great to me all afternoon. When she came back from class and found me crying my eyes out, she sat next to me and stroked my back until I was finished. Then she pulled me to my feet and marched me to the dining hall for dinner. Now she's engaged in a makeover, and I get the feeling she's wanted to do this for a while. Truth is, Jasmine's always been nice, but I didn't expect her to save me like this. I mean, sure, we're friends, but I never really got what she saw in me.

But now that we've been together all afternoon, and I've bawled my eyes out in front of her, asking doesn't seem so terrifying anymore. "Hey, Jasmine?"

"Yeah?"

"Why me?"

"Why you what? Why didn't Ben go for you? Girl, no one has any—"

"No, why are we friends?"

Jasmine stops and looks at me. I shake my head. "That sounds wrong. I mean, why are you being so nice to me?"

She frowns. "Why wouldn't I be?"

"Well, you're so *you*. You're pretty and, God, you've got it all figured out. You're like this confident, celebrity freshman and… Why me?"

Jasmine's quiet and my stomach churns. Why did I ask

that? Whatever we had going for us as friends I just blew to pieces by drawing attention to it. Looking at me in the mirror, she must be thinking, *Why* am *I friends with this sad, lost little girl?*

Finally, she says, "You know I started dating Sean when I was fifteen, right?"

"Yeah."

"We've been through a lot. We've both changed, and now it's college, and Sean is like, famous, when he should just be some sophomore. But despite that, he and I are the real thing."

I nod. "You totally are. He adores you, though I'm sure the football stuff is hard…"

"It's crazy," she says. "It's great that I get to go to all these parties and events with him. But here's the thing: since I've been here, not one person has talked to me because I'm *me*. All these girls want to hang with me and get to know the team or get close to Sean. Can you believe that shit?"

"Girls talk to you because they're after Sean?"

Jasmine rolls her eyes. "You have no idea. I can't trust anybody." Then our eyes meet in the mirror. "Except you."

My face warms. "Me?"

"You. From day one, you were just you. You're so damn serious, and so cute with this thing for Bookstore Boy. On the first day, you didn't even know who Sean was."

"So you like hanging with me because I'm ignorant?"

"No, that's why I *started* hanging with you. It was a relief to know you didn't want anything from me. But I *kept* hanging with you because I like you. You're smart. You're nice. And you want to be the best you can be. Just like me."

I laugh. "I'm *nothing* like you." Or Alex for that matter—

I'm nothing like these confident girls who know exactly what they want.

She chuckles and pats my shoulder. "So I know exactly who I want to be, and you're still figuring it out. So what? The point is we want to be the best."

Maybe she has a point. I don't know what I want to do with myself, but I want to make a difference. I want to be the best me I can be. So does she.

It wasn't enough for Ben, but Jasmine likes me just the way I am. And right now, when she's the only thing holding me together, I'm so grateful for her friendship.

An hour later, I'm second-guessing our friendship as she drags me up the steps to a huge, ramshackle house in the student ghetto. Chaotic music and voices boom out to the street. Light pours from every window.

"Are you sure about this?" I murmur, tugging at my shirt. Well, Jasmine's shirt. She let me wear my dark skinny jeans and my only nice pair of wedge heels, but decided none of my shirts would do and loaned me one of hers. It's some sort of tight, black, stretchy knit that looks great on me. Even my boobs look better in it, and they aren't generally much to look at. But now that we're about to head inside, I feel exposed and awkward.

"It'll be fine," Jasmine says.

"Whose party is this?"

She shrugs. "Not sure. Some guy in my humanities class gave me a flyer."

I gape at her. "Do we even know a single person here?"

She puts her arm around me and gently pulls me forward. "We will before the night's over. Come on! This is just what you need. A little music and a house full of strangers."

That sounds awful right now, but I don't say so.

"Let's just have a drink and dance, okay? It'll be fun." She tugs me up the wide wooden steps.

I grimace as I let her lead me inside. I'll just stay for an hour. One drink.

Chapter Twelve

BEN

I've been at this damn party for forty-five minutes, and there's no sign of Alex. She probably didn't even come, which pisses me the fuck off, and it's given me way too much time to think about what happened with Hannah earlier today, which isn't helping.

I've been arguing with myself about it all afternoon. On one hand, she fucking blew up at me like we were dating and she caught me cheating or some shit. We're friends, sure, but that doesn't mean she gets to know every part of my life.

On the other hand, she wasn't exactly wrong about what happened in her room last Friday—or what almost happened. I freaked out when we almost kissed, but I *wanted* to do it. Hell, I still kind of wish I had. So maybe that means I've been leading her on. I don't know anymore.

Maybe this is for the best. Things were getting too

complicated. Maybe it's better that we stop hanging out, although I hate the thought of that. Maybe that makes me selfish. Not that it matters, since like it or not, I'm pretty sure we're not speaking anymore.

Maybe I should fuck this stupid party and get drunk at home. Frankly, I'm halfway there, since I've been drinking tons of this punch shit they've got in red plastic cups just to have something to do. It's bright red and way too sweet, which means it's 80 percent grain alcohol, and I'll regret it in the morning. Oh the fuck well.

Then I see the swing of Alex's long, dark hair as she weaves through the crowd. I push past some people until there she is—holding some guy's hand.

She spots me at the same moment, and her face lights up. "Hey, Ben! You came."

I look from her to the guy she's with. He's at least six-two and seriously broad, with perfectly tousled blond hair and a square jaw. He's wearing a tidy white dress shirt and chinos. Jesus, he reminds me of my brother, Gavin. This is who she wants? No wonder we've been talking for a year without a spark. I'm the polar opposite of this guy.

"Yeah," I finally say. "I came."

She smiles. "This is Chip. Chip, this is Ben. He works at the bookstore across the street from Oasis."

Chip tilts his chin up in a vague bro nod. He scarcely registers my presence, which is about right with guys like him. I should know. I grew up with one.

He kisses Alex's cheek. "Hey, babe, I'm going to find a drink."

Chip heads off toward the kitchen, and Alex watches him go with stars in her eyes. All she's missing are little birds and hearts circling her damn head.

She's never even glanced at me like that. Maybe there's a reason that nothing's happened between us all this time.

Not that it matters now. Alex is taken. Out of my reach after I've been pursuing her for a year. But that's bullshit, right? My pursuit, if you can call it that, was always half-assed until today. Why did I suddenly decide to make my move on her? Maybe this wasn't about Alex at all. Maybe it was about Hannah and that almost-kiss last week.

Maybe that's why, standing here, I'm not even pissed. Just tired. Over it. Irritated.

"I didn't know you had a boyfriend."

She throws me a quick sheepish look and stares after Chip again. So she knew I was into her. She *knew* what this was about, and yet she still invited me here and played along like…

Fuck.

Like I did to Hannah. Not on purpose, granted, but still. Guess I can't say I don't deserve this.

"Yeah, Chip is great," she says. "After that mess with Brick, it's great to be with someone with a plan."

"Brick?"

"My ex." She shakes her head. "I have the worst taste in men. Really, it's tragic. First there was Brick, then that debacle with Marc."

"You were with *Marc*?"

She rolls her eyes and laughs. "Marc was just a drunken hookup, but yeah. Never sleep with guys from work. But I've finally figured it out with Chip. He's the one. He's smart and driven and he knows what he wants."

"Yeah, seems like it."

I am the biggest idiot on the planet. What the hell did I think I was doing? For all the time we've spent hanging out, I clearly know nothing about her life. And here I was buying her jewelry and declaring myself. I've been wasting my time and...

Jesus. Hannah was right, and not only that, I said some really shitty things to her because I *thought* I was hung up on this girl who is completely oblivious to me. I was a total asshole.

Alex is still talking, raving on and on about Chip and his MBA program, but I'm barely paying attention. Enough is enough. I have important things to think about. An important person. "Hey, Alex, I'm going to go."

She blinks. "But you just got here."

"Long day." I shrug. "I'll see you around."

Before she can stop me, I turn and shove my way through the crowd. More people have shown up. The whole house is packed. The voices, laughter, and pounding music throb in my ears. I get to the front hallway just as Hannah slips between two giant guys and stumbles to a stop in front of me.

I've never been happier to see someone as I am to see her. Everything in me goes light; my chest feels tight and my hands itch to touch her. I don't know how she's here, but she's *here*. This feeling... This was that look on Alex's face when she looked at Chip. And I *get it*.

God, I've been so stupid. She was right in front of me all along.

Hannah, however, doesn't look so happy to see me. She scowls. "Oh. It's you."

She looks different. Gorgeous. She's wearing makeup, her hair is curled, and her shirt— Damn, have her breasts always looked like that? She's also bleary-eyed and slurring and gripping a plastic red cup like a lifeline.

"Hey, Hannah," I say warily. "What are you doing here?"

"It's a party." She waves her cup to indicate the mass of bodies around us. Some of the artificially red punch sloshes out on her hand, but she doesn't notice. "Or wait. Are you asking why I'm not tucked up in bed at home like a good little girl?"

I roll my eyes. "Cut it out. You know that's not what I meant."

She takes a huge gulp of her drink, eying me over the edge of her cup. "I think that's exactly what you meant."

"How much of that have you had to drink?"

"None of your business."

"Who did you come here with?"

"Also none of your business."

Seriously? She's got a right to be mad at me, but she doesn't have to be so damn difficult about it. It's just a question. "Come on, Hannah. Are you here alone?"

She laughs bitterly. "No, I came with Jasmine."

"Where is she?"

Hannah waves her cup behind her, not spilling this time, but almost. "In there somewhere. I lost track of her. See, *she* knows I can take care of myself, because I'm not a child."

"Yeah? Well, you're being a lousy adult right now. Listen—"

Then some guy walks up behind her and slings his arm over her shoulders. "There you are. You got away from me." He's some preppy frat boy, and the way he's looking at Hannah, like she's his next meal, twists my stomach.

"I'm right here." She throws him a fake bright smile.

"I found that video I was telling you about. Come on

upstairs. My laptop's up there, and I'll show you."

My vision goes red. Adrenaline floods my system as every warning alarm sounds at once in my head. "Yeah, okay, no fucking way." I grab her wrist and pull her out from underneath his arm.

"Hey!" Hannah protests as I pluck her cup out of her hands and deposit it onto a nearby table.

"What the hell, man?" the douchey dude bro says, stepping toward me. He could probably kick my ass if he wanted to, but he looks drunker than Hannah, so I can handle him if I have to. I hope.

"Hey, man, the creepy date-rape thing isn't gonna happen tonight," I say.

Hannah shoves at my shoulder. "What do you think you're doing, Ben?"

I ignore her, take her by the arm, and turn her toward the door. "Taking you back to your dorm."

"What if I don't want to go?"

"I don't care. I'm not leaving you alone with that guy and whatever the fuck he's planning to try upstairs. I can guarantee he's not going to show you a funny cat video on YouTube."

She's still protesting, but I've got her outside now and down the steps. It's quieter, and without the noise and the liquor fueling her, the fight goes out of her. She slips her arm out of my grasp.

"Fine, I'm going. You don't need to babysit me. I'm sure you have better things to do. Better people to do, too."

I ignore the jab. "I'm not letting you walk across campus alone at this time of night."

She glowers at me but just turns and stomps off down

the sidewalk. I catch up to her in a few strides because she's wobbly in her heels and so much shorter than me. She ignores me as she types something on her phone.

"Who are you calling?"

"I'm texting Jasmine to let her know I left."

"Will she be okay?"

Hannah shrugs. "Sean was on his way."

"Right...Sean." Jasmine's linebacker boyfriend would have been handy to have around a few minutes ago when I was staring down Douchebag Doug back there.

Hannah huffs out a breath and glares at me. "I'll be okay, too. Seriously, you don't need to babysit me."

"I'm walking you back," I say stubbornly.

"I thought you had *plans*," she snaps.

Alex's tirade about Chip replays in my mind. "Nope. I most definitely do not have plans."

She sniffs. "Too bad."

I get that she's mad—and honestly, she has every right to be—but I don't like Hannah like this. I don't like that I made her like this.

"Hannah, can we talk—"

"No!" She speeds up. "I don't want to talk about anything. There's *nothing* to talk about."

"I think there is."

"No, there's not. It's pretty clear that there is absolutely nothing to talk about."

Fine. If she doesn't want to talk about it, I guess I can respect that. I don't press her further. "Did you finish the book?"

She barks out a hollow laugh. "Yeah, I did."

"What did you think?"

"Awesome. Brilliant. It changed my life. They all did."

"That's a good thing, isn't it?"

She shoots a sideways glance at me and then looks back at her feet. She's taller than usual in those heels, and the angle makes her calves curve differently. Her tight jeans stick to her legs like a second skin and hug her ass like—

"Sure, it's a good thing," she says, snapping me out of my inappropriate ogling. "You pointed me toward some amazing books that changed everything. So yeah, for what it's worth, thank you."

Something twists in my chest— Why is she talking like this is the last time she's going to see me?

Maybe because I told her it might be. My words from our fight come back to haunt me. I blew off what we had together and implied she didn't matter to me. I'm a dick. I thought pursuing Alex was the right thing, but all I did was hurt someone I care about.

I wish we could go back to how we were. I want her to come into the bookstore full of thoughts and feelings about what she's read, desperate to tell me all about it. But I fucked everything up, and I have no idea how to get back to that place, or if we even can.

"Are you going home for Thanksgiving?" I ask to break the silence.

"Yeah," she says softly. We're at the edge of campus now, and she doesn't sound angry anymore. Tired and sad more like it, but at least she's not pissed. "My dad is coming to get me tomorrow night. You?"

She's not biting my head off, so that's something, I guess. "Yeah. I'm not driving back until Thursday morning, though. Trying to minimize my time in the cross hairs." Her eyes

flicker to mine because she knows going home sucks for me.
But then she just looks away.

"Are you going to tell your dad about chemistry?" I ask.

"I don't want to talk about it."

"Hannah, I know it's eating at you, but he sounds really
understanding. I'm sure if you just talk to him—"

"I said I don't want to talk about it," she snaps with an
icy finality. I guess we don't share like that anymore. I didn't
realize how much I'd gotten used to discussing this stuff with
her. She was the only person I could talk to about my family,
and now she's gone.

When we get to her dorm, Hannah fumbles through her
jean pockets for her key card. It's no wonder she has trouble
getting the card— Those pants are *really* tight. Not that I'm
complaining. She has great legs…

She finally produces her key card and promptly drops it.

"Stop." I hold up my hand. "I got it."

She sighs and leans against the doorframe while I grab
it and swipe us in.

"You can come up, but just to the door. No assholes al-
lowed inside," she says over her shoulder as we walk back to
the elevators.

Ignoring the insult, I follow her in and punch six for her
floor. She slouches against the far wall of the elevator and
watches me warily. Her eye makeup is a little smudged, but
it makes her look kind of sultry. I shift uncomfortably. Every
time I look at her, I find something else I can't stop staring
at.

"Do you have aspirin?" I ask.

"What?"

"Aspirin. You should take some and drink all the water

you can manage."

The elevator doors ding open, and she forges ahead into the hallway. "Why?"

"It'll help with your hangover tomorrow."

She snorts and punches in the code to unlock the door to her room. "I won't be hungover."

"That stuff was mostly vodka. You'll be hungover."

"Fine." She pushes the door open and walks into her dark room. The overhead lights are off, but the twinkle lights strung up over her bed are on. "I'll take my aspirin and drink my water." Not two steps in, the semi-darkness swallows her, and she trips over something.

"Hannah—" I'm inside before I know it and, somehow, manage to catch her before she hits the ground.

As soon as she's back on her feet, she swats my hands away. "I'm fine, I'm fine." She spins around and pokes me in the chest. "So the babysitting is done now." I can barely make out her features in the low light, but her choked voice is impossible to miss. She sniffles, and my stomach sinks— Is she crying?

I gently hold her upper arms. "Hannah…"

"No!" This time there's no mistaking the way her voice cracks. "Why are you even here? You're not interested in me, remember? You want *Alex*. Quit fussing over me like you're my big brother."

I wince. "I'm not your brother." She scoffs and starts to step back, but I pull her closer.

"No, you're not," she whispers. She's so close.

"Hannah—"

She leans in, and her warm breath on my neck sends a chill racing up my spine, across my scalp. "And I'm *not* a little girl."

"I know you're not." Jesus, do I know it.

What the fuck am I doing? What are *we* doing? It's dark, I'm holding on to her, and she's leaning into me. Our hot, whispered words fall into this tiny, electrified space between us. She looks up at me, and my gaze catches on her mouth. Her full upper lip is like sin. I've been trying so hard to be polite, to be a gentleman, but God, I want to know how her mouth feels and how she'd look if I pulled that tight shirt off her. I want to touch her smooth skin and wrap her silky hair around my fingers.

But I can't. She's drunk and pissed, and this is such a bad idea. I should go before I do something stupid. I shouldn't be —

And then her mouth is on mine, and *she* is kissing *me,* and all thinking stops, like a bomb just went off in my brain. My mouth moves over hers. Her lips part and her tongue brushes my bottom lip, urging me to meet her halfway. I can't help it. I touch her tongue with mine, shuddering when she gasps into my mouth. Her hands fist into my shirt, then slide up, her nails scraping my neck. Her fingers slide into my hair, and I moan — It feels so good.

I move one hand up to her neck, and her long, glossy hair falls over my fingers. I grip the back of her neck as we kiss — deeper, harder, more. My other hand slips down to her ass and grips her tightly. Her hips press into me — Jesus, I'm so hard.

She stumbles backward, pulling me with her. It isn't far; just a few steps and her legs hit the edge of her bed. We tumble down until she's on her back, and I'm lying over her.

In the dreamlike near-dark, I get lost in her mouth, the

feel of her lips and tongue, the scrape of her teeth on my lip. God, she feels incredible under me. My head spins as I find her breast. It fills my palm perfectly. I stroke my thumb across her nipple, and her back arches up off the bed, pressing into me, so I do it again. I slide my hand up under her shirt, touching her smooth, warm skin, cupping her again with just the lace of her bra between us.

She grinds against me, and my dick presses between her legs. She wraps her legs around my hips— Her calves hook on to my thighs as we press against each other.

"Ben," she whispers, fisting her hands into my hair.

My hips flex in response and I groan. My fingers find the button of her jeans, fumbling between our bodies. I don't want clothes. I don't want anything between us. My heart races, and her skin under my fingers is so hot. I pull down the zipper on her jeans and—

Crap.

I yanked her out of that party to get her away from the creepy date-rape dude, and here I am about to cross a serious line with Hannah. Hell, we've already crossed a line. Four or five of them. They're about a mile back, scorched and smoking. It'd be so easy to take this the whole way.

Being with her feels so wonderful, so *right*, but I don't want it to happen like this, both of us drunk, Hannah still angry.

Even though it's the last thing I want to do, I pull back. When I stand up, I stagger— Right, I'm a little drunk, and Hannah is a *lot* drunk. This is wrong on so many levels.

"Ben, what—"

"Sorry," I blurt out. "I'm really sorry. That was wrong. I shouldn't have done that."

She sits up. In the dim light, I can just make out her hair, a tangled mess from my hands, and her shirt, pushed up and askew. "It's okay. I wanted you to."

"And I want to. But not like this."

She rolls her eyes and crosses her arms over her chest. "Of course not. God forbid you do something you'll regret tomorrow."

Of course she's misinterpreting me. Why shouldn't she? I've got some serious making up to do. I sit next to her and cup her cheek with my palm, then turn her face to mine. Her eyes can barely focus— Sleeping together tonight would've been a seriously bad decision.

"No, I don't want it to be something *you* regret. I'd like you to remember it, and right now, I'm pretty sure you won't. Maybe we'd better try this again when we're both sober."

She scowls adorably. "You mean you're not sorry?"

I chuckle and run my thumb over her cheekbone. "No, I'm not sorry."

"Wow," she mutters, almost to herself. "Jasmine was right."

"Jasmine?"

"She said I should make the first move because you never would."

"Yeah, I definitely needed a kick upside the head about this." I brush some hair off her face and hook it behind her ear. "Look, sleep it off tonight, and we'll talk tomorrow before we leave for the weekend, okay? I'm going to get you some water." I press a kiss to her forehead, and she nods wearily.

I get up, find their mini dorm fridge in the dark, and grab a bottle of water, but when I turn back to the bed, Hannah's toppled to her side and she's sound asleep.

With a sigh, I set the water on the nightstand where she can find it later, take off her shoes, and pull the quilt over her. She'll be in a world of hurt tomorrow, but hopefully after that, we can make everything better.

Just as I leave her dorm and close the door, my cell buzzes in my pocket. Who would message me this late at night?

Dad. Of course. Not who I want to talk to. But even he can't tarnish how wonderful tonight was. I swipe my finger across the phone and open his text.

Chapter Thirteen

HANNAH

The sunlight pouring through the windows is absolutely blinding when Jasmine shuts the door behind her, waking me up. I groan and close my eyes, smothering my face with the pillow. My mouth feels full of cotton.

Jasmine drops her bag onto her bed. "What happened to you last night?"

"I texted you about going home."

"Yeah, but why? When I went to get a drink, you were dancing in the living room with Mr. Alpha Sigma Frat Boy. You looked like you were having fun. Or relaxing, at least."

"He was kind of gross," I mutter. The preppy boy with those stupid plaid shorts and the drunken leer swims through my foggy mind. I think he kissed me. I'm pretty sure it was wet and unpleasant.

"So you ran out of there?"

"No, I ran into Ben." And just like that, the rest of the night floods back in. Arguing with Ben at the party, arguing with Ben as he marched me home, arguing with Ben as he insisted on taking me straight to the door. Then a dark room, and his hands, and kissing, and the bed, and Ben on top of me in the dark—

"Oh, God." I slap my hands over my face.

"Uh-oh." Jasmine crosses to my bed and perches on the edge. "What happened?"

"He walked me home."

"And?"

"And... I'm not sure what happened. Jesus, I was so drunk." Ugh, Ben was right— I was *way* too drunk to make any decisions last night. Thank God he got me away from that creepy guy, too.

"So..." Jasmine prompts. "You were drunk. And something happened."

"We kissed."

Her eyes go wide. "Ohhh-kay. You weren't kidding. How did that happen? Who kissed who? Did he kiss you or did you kiss him?"

"I'm not sure. One minute we weren't and the next minute we were." My face flames— *Did* I initiate it? Did I just throw myself at him? Oh, God. "I was so mad at him, and he was being so bossy, still treating me like his kid sister. And then..."

"You don't kiss your kid sister."

"You don't do the other stuff, either."

Jasmine gasps. "Hannah. Did you...?"

"No. Not that. But we did more than kiss." Ben's hands on my body, under my shirt, unzipping my jeans—

My face burns, and I groan into my hands. I can't believe

I did that.

"Shit," she says.

"Yeah, shit. Especially since I'm pretty sure I passed out in the middle of it. God, I practically mauled him."

"Oh, no! Hannah…" Jasmine reaches for me, but I wave her hands away, too humiliated for consolation just yet. I just want to melt into the blankets, never to be heard of again. *Hannah Gregory? Yeah, she used to go here until she literally died of embarrassment.*

I bury my face in my pillow. "I should move somewhere," I say. "An island. Far away. Where no one can find me."

Jasmine laughs, which gets me giggling a little, too.

"What happened?" she says.

I start to respond, but then my phone rings. Jasmine grabs it off my nightstand, and when she looks at the face, her eyes light up.

"It's him."

"Oh, God, no."

As if I wasn't humiliated enough. The only thing worse than what I did last night is having to talk about it the next day.

"Do you want me to answer?" Jasmine asks, finger poised over the screen. "I'm really good at ripping guys a new one. I'll do it for you if you want."

She actually looks like she's relishing the possibility, but that wouldn't be right. I got myself into this mess; I have to dig myself out.

"No, I'll talk to him."

Reluctantly, she turns over the phone. "I'll go get us some coffee. I'm guessing you could really use it."

"Thanks."

As the door shuts behind her, I swipe my finger across the screen to answer Ben's call. "Hey."

But instead of Ben's voice, there's a loud crackle of what sounds like wind.

"Ben? Are you there?"

The wind gets fainter, then cuts off. "Sorry, had the window down."

"The window? Are you driving?"

He pauses. "Yeah. I'm sorry. My dad sent me a text last night and said I have to come home a day early for Thanksgiving. Apparently, he has great news that can't wait."

I sit onto my bed. "You don't sound too excited about it."

"Oh, I'm excited. Super. Excited." He laughs at his humorless joke, and I laugh with him. We've got the ability to joke about our misery, at least. "Seriously, though, my dad has a terrible idea of what constitutes good news. Nothing good will come of this weekend."

"You'll be okay," I say.

"Yeah. But listen. That's not why I called. I needed you to know…"

I lean back onto the bed, and a flash of last night pops into my mind. His hands on me, under my shirt, going higher— I groan. "You really don't have to do this."

"Do what?"

"Let me down easy or whatever. It's really fine. I'm fine." My face is on fire. If I have to sit here and listen to him explain that he likes me as a friend but he just doesn't see me that way, I swear I won't survive it.

"That's not what I was going to say."

"Because you were right. I was really drunk and had no idea what I was doing, so we can just move on and forget it ever happened—"

"I don't want to forget it. Not what happened at the café. And definitely not what happened last night."

My heart leaps. "You don't?"

"I told you so last night, but apparently you lost that one to the vodka."

I can barely breathe. I thought Ben was calling to brush me off politely and awkwardly, but that's not what he's saying. I swallow thickly, scrambling for something to say, but it's like he opened a dam, and the words keep spilling out of him.

"Last night I'd already had this…epiphany, I guess, and then you were there, and everything went crazy, and now I can't stop thinking about it."

"What about Alex?"

"That was the epiphany. She's not the one I want."

Everything in me goes still, except for my heart, which is trying to pound its way right out of my chest. "And… I am?"

"Yeah—" He says something else, but his voice cuts in and out.

"Ben? Can you still hear me?"

His voice comes back into focus. "…don't want to forget last night. How do you feel about that?"

"Umm…"

I'm dying here. Why did his dad have to tell him to come home a day early? Why did Ben have to go? If we were standing in front of each other, this would be so much easier. No stupid broken phone signal to cut off half of what he's saying, and no distance between us to keep me from shutting him up and kissing him again.

"Is that a good 'umm' or a bad 'umm'?" he asks.

"It's good." My face warms. "It's really good."

"I think it's good, too." God, we sound like a couple of idiots, speaking in sounds and sighs and dopey half-sentences. But I don't care. Ben and I might be on the way to something, and I can't wait to see him again and find out what it is.

Jasmine knocks on the door and pokes her head in. She sees me on the phone and mouths, "Oops."

I shake my head and gesture for her to come back inside.

"I should let you go," I say.

"Yeah, I should get off the phone and focus on the road. But I had to call you."

There's a long pause, and I frown— Did the phone call cut off completely? But then he speaks again.

"Hannah, listen. I know things are weird between us right now. Just… Don't disappear on me. I want to see you after break and figure this out."

My heart melts. There's a lot left for us to figure out. I don't know exactly where we stand or where we're going, but at least we're going to try.

"I'd like that." It's a stupendous understatement. I'm so giddy right now, I feel like I could fly straight through the roof.

We say good-bye and hang up. Jasmine stares at me, clutching two coffee cups so hard she's about to crush them. She sets them carefully onto the nightstand and plants her hands onto her hips.

"That didn't sound like a brush off," she says.

"It wasn't." I can't keep the ridiculous grin off my face. "Not at all."

She claps her hands together. "Oh, I'm going to need *all* the details about *that* conversation. Pull yourself together, Vodka Girl. We're going to have full-on boy crazy girl talk right now over breakfast."

"No, please."

"Are you hungover?"

"Horribly." Damn it, Ben was right about that, too. This would be so much easier if I could lord just one thing over him.

"So we're going to get you loaded up on caffeine and greasy food. You'll feel much better. Trust me."

"I'm not sure I want to feel better," I moan pathetically. Isn't that terrible? But it's true. Last night was wonderful. Yeah, my head hurts like hell, but the pain is a kind of reminder of last night. It was real. It happened, and now every little twitch makes me think of Ben and his lips and his hands and his—

"Girl, you have got it *bad*." Jasmine grabs my hands and hauls me upright. "Come on. Your dad is getting here tonight, so you have to shake off this hangover." Her gaze rakes over me. "And frankly, you look pretty rough."

I take a deep breath, stand, and brace myself as the room tilts slightly. "Okay," I say with more conviction than I feel. "Breakfast. Let's do it."

"That's my girl. Let's go show the world that they haven't seen the best of Hannah Gregory yet."

My head is spinning as I pull myself together, and not just from the hangover. So much is happening. I'm facing a long holiday weekend with my dad when I'm keeping so many things from him. Ben's also facing a long weekend that'll be difficult for him in a totally different way. And then there's "us," or what might become "us," once we see each other again. The rest is unpleasant, but *that*? I can hardly wait.

Chapter Fourteen

*B*EN

I've been home for one day, and I'm already ready to kill someone, starting with my dad and followed shortly thereafter by my brother. I should be with Hannah, trying to figure out what's going on between us. Instead, I'm spending the stupid holiday at my family's place so Dad can share his "great news." Somehow, I get the feeling he's the only one who will have something to be thrilled about.

He still hasn't even told me, in spite of dragging me home a day early to do it. He spent all day yesterday at his office, and I didn't even see him until after nine. He probably commanded my presence in Columbus just to prove his power over me. That'd be just like him.

And now the whole family is settled around the table in our cold, overly-formal dining room, and he still hasn't said anything. I'm so over his Sun Tzu *Art of War* psychological bullshit.

"So, what do you think of the Bengals' chances this year, buddy?" Dad asks Gavin.

Dad and Gavin don't just share a love of football that borders on obsession; they look exactly alike, too—tall, broad-shouldered, blond, ruddy-faced. Gav even talks like Dad, in this too-loud, too-slick salesman's voice. They both charge through life like they have to convince everyone of their own dominance.

I feel like I'm shrinking whenever I'm in the same room with them, like everything I thought I knew about myself disappears. Ironically, they're what pushed me to books in the first place— Reading has always been my escape.

Gavin leans back in his chair and smiles, so stupidly pleased with himself for no reason at all. "They'd be a lot better if they hadn't traded Armstrong for that Kirkpatrick kid."

My dad shakes his head sadly. "Damn shame."

Mom sighs as she refills her wine glass. "Can we save the football talk for after dinner?"

"You'll spend the rest of the day watching it. Surely you can hold off talking about it for an hour," Aunt Lisa—Mom's sister—says. Her husband left her to marry his secretary six years ago, and Aunt Lisa has never stopped being angry with Mom for still having a husband, which Mom passive-aggressively lords over her. They communicate with fake smiles and sublimated rage.

"All these years, and the boys are still obsessed with football." Mom laughs, then evidently remembers she's talking about my dad and Gavin, not me. Her eyes flicker to me momentarily, and she bites her lip and shifts in her seat.

Nobody else notices. Dad and Gavin are plowing through huge plates of food, and my vapid cousin, Megan, hasn't said a word since we sat down. She's too busy pouting because her mom made her put her phone away at the table.

"Everything is delicious, Jess," Aunt Lisa says insincerely.

"I went with a new place this year. They worked out well."

Mom means the caterer who made Thanksgiving dinner. My mother doesn't cook. She finds the very idea distasteful. She's not crazy about eating, either. Mostly, she pushes her food around with her fork and nibbles between sips of chardonnay.

"Gav," my dad says, trying again. "How's the training program going?"

"Pretty good. Got to have lunch with Murphy and Reynolds last week. They're pretty big in the firm."

"Good, good. Make sure they know how eager you are. Show 'em what you've got. That's how you get ahead."

So Gavin gets ahead by brown-nosing a couple of financial bigwigs over beers while I read hundreds of pages a week and write essay after essay about them, all with stellar grades, but *I'm* the one wasting my life.

I down the rest of my beer and grab another from the fridge, surprising the hell out of the poor woman from the catering company dealing with our dinner. Does she have a family at home having Thanksgiving dinner without her while she serves our miserable household? I return silently to the table and keep my eyes on my beer. Maybe if I don't say anything, everyone will forget I'm here, and I'll get out of this dinner unscathed.

God, I wish I was anywhere but here. Like in Hannah's room, a week ago, eating extra cheese pizza. I should have kissed her that night— I *wanted* to kiss her that night, even if I was in denial. And then I *did* kiss her two nights ago, and Jesus, why was I trying so hard not to? Tangled on her bed in the dark, kissing, touching, and on the way to doing a whole lot more. It was amazing. *She's* amazing.

After how badly I handled everything, it's a miracle Hannah's even giving me the time of day. And instead of spending yesterday with her, figuring out how we're going to go forward, I wasted it in Columbus because my dad needed to remind me he's boss.

Thinking about Hannah makes me imagine her here and… Ugh, Dad would be *delighted* with that choice. Three years younger than me and pursuing a science degree because she wants to help sick people. I can almost hear my dad's dismissive "soft-hearted, hippie bullshit" comment.

"How are the grades holding up, sport?" Dad's voice jars me. He's called me "sport" and Gavin "buddy" as long as I can remember, even though I've never played sports of any kind. I guess in his mind, Gavin and I are the matched set he always hoped for and still can't believe he didn't get.

"Fine. As good as they've always been. Still carrying a three point nine GPA." I pass the potatoes to Aunt Lisa.

"Megan could stand to learn a few things about applying herself like Ben does," Aunt Lisa says. Megan's in her senior year of high school and shows about as much enthusiasm for college as she might for a root canal. She doesn't even glance up when her mom starts talking about her. It's hard to believe that Megan is just a year younger than Hannah. They come from different worlds entirely. I've always known Hannah was exceptional, but it's made clear when I compare her to Megan.

"Go easy on her, Lisa," my dad says. "The kids all have to sow some wild oats when they're young."

Aunt Lisa sighs and shakes her head. "Steve, you're so lucky Ben is such a good student."

My dad snorts dismissively. "He'd better be a good student, since all he does is read."

I swallow down a flush of rage and force myself to speak calmly. "My last paper was about the role agnosticism plays in Thomas Hardy's works. There's a bit more involved than just *reading*."

"You know what your dad meant." Mom laughs. I'm pretty sure she's the one who doesn't know what Dad meant. Or rather, she doesn't want to know. I don't respond. It's pointless. This is Thanksgiving, and I'm trying really hard to get through the day without an ugly scene.

"It's fine." Dad gestures expansively. "You can afford to be a little frivolous with your undergrad degree as long as you knuckle down after that and go into something that'll earn you a decent living."

"I could make money with an English degree," I protest.

"That shitty little bookstore job isn't going to cut it, and you know it."

"I won't work there forever. Actually…" I swallow hard. I can't believe I'm about to say this out loud. "If I got my PhD, I could teach. College."

He throws his head back and laughs. *Laughs*. My face goes hot, and my stomach churns— This was such a bad idea. Why did I open my mouth?

"That's just an excuse to spend your life in school instead of finding a real job," Dad says.

Gavin smirks. "Let us know when you're ready to pull

your head out of your ass and join the real world, Ben."

"So I can spend all day selling electronic shares in a bunch of imaginary shit like you?"

"Hey," Dad snaps. "That industry put a roof over your head and money in your pockets. Now it's time to pay it back, kid. I was fine when you didn't want to follow in the family business. I was fine when you decided to major in English, but you're in your final year, and it's time to make some plans."

"If this is about law school—"

Gavin scoffs softly. "Yeah, sure. Ben's going to law school."

Dad points his fork at Gavin, then at me. "You're damn right he's going to law school."

"I'm just not sure law school is the right fit for me," I mutter.

"What's the matter, Ben?" Gavin chuckles. "Don't think you can hack it?"

"I could fucking ace law school compared to you, moron."

Dad smiles smugly, sets his fork down, and leans forward onto his elbows. "That's just the kind of attitude I like hearing from you, sport. You're going to need that drive next year at the Chicago College of Law— It's one of the best in the country. When you get out, top notch firms will be lining up to recruit you."

This is it—his big news—and I just wandered right into it. I clear my throat. "There's no way I can get into a program like that."

"With a little help, which I just so happen to have access to, you sure can. An old fraternity buddy of mine is on the faculty there. I shot him an email and told him how eager you were to get into the program, and he's happy to coach you through the process."

"Isn't that exciting?" Mom trills.

"That'll give you quite an edge, Ben," Aunt Lisa says bitterly.

"I don't think—"

But Dad charges along like I didn't speak. "He's already emailed you the application and some pointers. You have to write some kind of essay, but you should be able to ace that part, right, sport? All those English classes will finally come in handy."

I start to protest that I never got an email, but Dad must have given this guy my old Gmail address from when I was in high school. I never gave my parents the Arlington State.edu address when I started school. The less access my dad has to me, the better.

"That sounds great, but—"

"No 'buts.'" Dad points his fork at me again. "Richard doesn't have to help you out— He's doing it as a favor to me. I expect you to get that application in ASAP."

Gavin snorts. "This should be fun."

"Shut up, asshole."

"Boys!" Mom snaps. All the tendons are standing out on her neck. "Can we just settle down and enjoy a nice family dinner?" She's clutching her wineglass so tightly her knuckles have gone white. There's a moment of tense silence at the table while Gavin and I glare at each other. Mom gulps down her wine, Dad glowers at me, Aunt Lisa smirks smugly, and Megan stares blankly into space.

Happy Thanksgiving.

Thanksgiving dinner in the Fisher house has always felt like the Bataan Death March, and I lost my appetite the second Dad threw down his "awesome news." But eventually, dessert is over and the plates are cleared.

Gavin grabs a beer and escapes to the family room to watch the game while Mom and Aunt Lisa snipe at each other. Megan retrieves her phone with a relieved sigh and resumes texting everyone she knows. As soon as Dad follows Gav into the den to scream obscenities at the TV all afternoon, I grab my coat and slip out of the house. I can't stand another minute of it. I walk through the sunny, cold, well-manicured streets of New Albany to try to clear my head, but it doesn't work.

It's Thanksgiving in the Columbus suburbs, which means it's freezing and almost nothing is open. I end up at a Starbucks, nursing a hot chocolate, just so I don't have to walk around outside. There's one sullen high school kid manning the register, and, impossibly, he looks even more miserable than me.

My laptop is in my messenger bag, and out of curiosity, I fire it up and log back into my old email account. It's been ages. There are a bunch of Facebook notifications—I still have a Facebook?—and a few emails from high school people I never gave my college email to. And there it is, halfway down the page, an email from Richard Parker, Esq., with the subject "Law school." I skim through it, and sure enough, Richard's willing to waltz me through the admissions process. It would be so easy.

I close out of my old email and open another document on my desktop: my application to Arlington State's master's program in English Lit. It's all filled out. I did it weeks ago, when Donnelly first said he wanted me in the program, but I still haven't sent it because I have no idea how I could possibly make it work.

Maybe it's because my dad makes me so fucking frustrated and furious, and I just need this act of rebellion. Maybe it's because after an afternoon of being invisible, unless I'm being told how to live my life, I just need to reclaim something that's me. Whatever it is, after staring at that application for weeks, I send it off to the admissions office in less than thirty seconds. The high of hitting send lasts another thirty seconds, until I remember I'm sitting in a Starbucks on Thanksgiving, hiding from my family, and I feel horrible again.

I want to talk—actually *talk*—to someone. I could call John, but while we've been good friends since freshman year, we don't really confide in each other about stuff like this. He knows I don't get along with my family, but that's the extent of it.

But Hannah knows all about my family. Maybe more than anyone who isn't related to me.

I scroll back to her name. I hate this kind of hesitation, the high school game of wondering what she'll think if I text, or if I should call. Should I wait until I get back to campus? Will I seem too eager if I text her now? Worse, my dad just gave me a big fat reminder about what's waiting for me in the future, and it's hard to see how this new thing with Hannah fits into it.

Maybe it's selfish, but I open up a text to her anyway

and type five words.

I miss talking to you.

Shit. I shouldn't have sent that— Could I be any sappier? But she answers back right away.

I miss talking to you, too.

Fuck this. Before I lose my nerve, I press call. She answers after the first ring.

"Hey." Her voice is soft but excited.

"Hey."

I swallow hard and rub my palm down my thigh. My hands are sweating even though it's thirty degrees outside. God, I've missed hearing her voice. How did she get buried so deeply in my life so fast? "How've you been?"

It seems impossible that it's been just over a day since that night in her dorm room. It feels like years. "Fine."

"How's your Thanksgiving?"

"It's good."

I hesitate. Last we spoke, she was freaked out about the questions her dad might ask about her major that she didn't know how to answer anymore. "What about your dad?"

"It's...okay."

"Have you told him about Honors Chem yet?"

She sighs. "Can we not talk about this?"

"Sure. Yeah." I can't blame her— I don't really want to talk about my family, either. I cast around for something less touchy to ask her, something about us. "You reading anything right now?"

"Yeah, I picked it up at World of Books yesterday, but it

sucks. It's so dumb."

This—*this*—is what I missed, being the one to give her books, staying up half the night talking about different stories with her. I want to have that again more than anything else, at least for a little while longer.

"World of Books?" I groan. That place is soulless—like Starbucks for books. "You're killing me."

"Well, there's that one right near campus—"

"I know, I know. Sorry it sucks."

"Me, too. But it didn't feel right going back to Prometheus without you there. I don't want anyone else to help me find a book."

My heart soars, and we're getting into a groove now where it feels natural to give her a hard time. "So you went to the soulless corporation instead? Hannah, that's probably the sweetest thing anyone's ever said to me."

She laughs loudly and freely, and the sound fills me with warmth. When she finally comes down, she asks, "How's your holiday?"

"Well, I'm sitting in a Starbucks right now, so that should tell you how it's going."

"Your family didn't do dinner?"

"Oh, no, Mom had it catered. The food wasn't the problem. It was the people."

"What happened?"

"My dad. You know, the usual. Going off about how I'm wasting my time and I'm an idiot and law school is my only option."

Hannah snorts dismissively. "Well, that's ridiculous. As soon as he sees how well you're doing working on your master's next year, he'll realize he was wrong."

I smile at her absolute confidence in me, even after everything that happened last week. I want to believe in her vision for next year, but I'm torn between what I want and what's *right*. Maybe I can figure out a way to make it happen, to make that application I just sent my reality.

"We'll see," I say.

"So was it really bad?"

"I'm sitting in a Starbucks, remember?"

"Right. Wow. What are you going to do?"

I sigh. "I think I'm just gonna grab my stuff and head back to Arlington."

"Tonight?"

"Yeah. I was going back early tomorrow anyway for work, Black Friday and all. But if I leave now, we won't get into any more fights."

She hesitates. "Are you going to be okay?"

"I'll be fine. Thanks, Hannah."

"For what?"

"Just…talking to me. I really needed this."

I needed it—her—more than I realized. We've got this whole other aspect to our relationship still waiting to be explored, but for now? I'm insanely happy to have this back.

"Hey, are you coming back to school on Sunday?" I ask.

"Yeah, Sunday afternoon."

"I'm working all day, but can I come see you when I get off? We should talk."

Neither of us says anything with the implication of "talk" hovering between us. We're going to talk, but there's some other unresolved business between us, too. Business that starts with kissing and ends where we both wanted it to go after the party.

"Yeah, we probably should," she says. "Come see me when you get off work."

Sunday feels like a century from now. This is sure to be the longest weekend I've ever lived through.

"Okay. Hannah?"

"Yeah?"

"Thanks for giving me another chance."

She giggles. "Oh, God."

"What?"

"It's *Thanksgiving*. What else could I do?" I laugh, too, until she interrupts me, her voice much more serious. "But I'd have given you another chance no matter what day it was, Ben."

It's official. I don't deserve this girl. "I won't let you down," I promise her.

It's only after I hang up that I realize I might have made a promise I can't keep.

Chapter Fifteen

My dad lingers forever when he's dropping me off at the dorm Sunday afternoon. Thanksgiving break was rough. Not Dad— Dad's always great. The hard part was keeping up this front that everything is fine.

There's a chance that things are still fine. A slim one. Right now, I'm failing chem. *Failing*. Technically, if I ace the final, I can pull out a passing grade, but I haven't aced anything so far, so I'm not holding my breath.

All that hard work and potential and I'm falling apart. Even if I manage to pass the class, I'll be out of the Honors Program. And the worst thing is the possibility of leaving the program doesn't upset me like it should. If anything, it'd be a relief. The choice I'm terrified to make would make itself.

For the whole long weekend, I tried to tell Dad, but the words lodged in my throat. So I didn't tell him, and now I'm back at school, still pretending everything is okay.

Is this what it's like for Ben? At least my dad isn't an asshole about it, which kind of makes me feel even worse. If he were mean, it'd be so much easier to forget about how disappointed he'll be in me. *Hey, Dad, remember all that work and all those years you poured into me, preparing me for my amazing future as a scientist? Never mind.*

Ugh. My heart hurts just imagining that conversation.

I'm desperate for Dad to leave so I can escape this guilt and anxiety and so I can see Ben. Maybe I'm being irresponsible, running to Ben so I don't have to deal with this big, unpleasant reality, but I don't care. Ever since he called me on Thanksgiving, I've been practically crawling out of my skin waiting to see him again.

"Did you get everything out of the trunk?" Dad runs a hand through his hair, which he's always worn a little long and shaggy, both for a chemist and a dad.

"Yeah, Dad."

"And the backseat?"

"Yep."

"Your coat, too? It was back there—"

"Dad. I got it."

He gives me a sheepish smile. "You're ready for me to clear out now, aren't you?"

"No! It's not that. I just kinda want to go see my friends."

"Friends? Any *particular* friend? Maybe the friend you've been electronically connected to all weekend?" He's teasing me. There's a smile dancing around the corners of his mouth.

I roll my eyes. "Maybe."

"Okay, okay, I'm going." He pats his pockets for his keys

and turns slowly in a circle, looking for anything he might be forgetting. My dad is brilliant but so absent-minded he's practically a hazard to himself. Without Mom, I had to step up early to keep the two of us and our house on track. I worry about him sometimes, now that I've left for college.

He finds his keys, a flicker of triumph crossing his face, and then he turns serious. "Be safe, okay? Call me if you need anything."

My smile fades as heat crawls up the back of my neck. "I will. Don't worry."

"A parent's default setting is worry, Hannah. But I trust you. I know you'll be just fine."

I have to tell him. And I will, just not today, not when Ben is here, a few blocks away. We hug again, he kisses the top of my head, presses a twenty into my hand, and then he's gone.

And so am I. The door barely clicks behind him before I tear through my room, brush my hair, slick on a little pink lipstick and a bit of mascara, and chomp on a breath mint — just in case.

Oh please let there be an in case...

I shrug back into my coat and fly out of my dorm. Ben said he'd come over after he gets off work, but that's still four hours away, and I'm going to go out of my mind waiting until then. We texted all weekend, but now I need more than words. I need him.

Coming into Prometheus feels like coming home. It's warm and smells of dust and old paper. It's a scent I associate viscerally with Ben— When I inhale deeply, my body tingles.

I find Ben behind the register, squinting at his computer screen, eyebrows furrowed in concentration, his face bathed in blue light. This weekend and all the things he said still feel like a dream. I'm half expecting him to look up and smile at me like a friend—make out session forgotten—before picking out another book for me to read.

But when Ben looks up, the smile that explodes across his face reassures me that everything he said this weekend was real. He's not looking at me like a friend.

"Hey," I say.

"Hey. When did you get back?"

"Just now."

He grins and slides from behind the register. I cross the front of the store, and we stop awkwardly, a foot apart. What should we do? Where should we touch? *Can* we even do anything here, in the middle of the store?

"Is Adele here?" I whisper.

"Upstairs, organizing the kids' books," he whispers back.

"Oh." I can't help the smile that spreads across my face.

He shouts back over his shoulder and in the general direction of the upstairs loft. "I'll be in the back, Adele. Keep an eye on the register?"

"Okay." Her voice floats down, faint and far away. "Don't do anything I wouldn't do!"

And here we thought we were going to get away with it.

Ben chuckles and grabs my hand before pulling me to the back of the store, down the aisle with ethics and philosophy. Nobody ever comes down this aisle. He stops and faces me, just inches away. It's kind of dim back here, since there's been a bulb burned out for ages and no one's bothered to replace it.

"Hey," Ben says again, but this time his voice is different. Low and private. He takes my other hand in his and laces our fingers together, palm-to-palm.

Something ignites in me, and I take a step closer. "Hey," I whisper.

"I missed you," he says. It makes my heart light up like a candle.

"I missed you, too."

"Hannah?"

"Yeah?"

"Do you want to go out sometime?"

And it's so ridiculous that he's asking me out on a date after everything—all the time we've spent together, the phone call this weekend, everything he said, and the intense make out session we already had. I giggle. "Really? A date?"

"Hey," he protests. "I'm trying to do this right. You have a better idea?"

I release his fingers and wrap my hands around his wrists. God, I love his wrists. Then I slide my hands up his arms to his surprisingly solid shoulders. His hoodie, my favorite worn navy blue one, is soft under my fingers, and he smells so good, like hot chocolate and old books, which has to be the best smell to ever exist. "How about you just kiss me?"

He cradles my face in his hands. "That works, too, I guess."

His lips touch mine, a soft, gentle exploration. He's kissing me like this is our first kiss. Because it should have happened just like this, in this dark aisle in this magic bookstore, with this boy I'm pretty sure I'm already in love with.

Chapter Sixteen

After Hannah leaves, the rest of the day drags by. It seems like forever before I close up the store and head to campus to meet her. My stomach churns with excitement and nerves. My hands are clammy, and my heart races every time I think of seeing her again. Our phone call on Thanksgiving and the texting for the rest of the weekend was great, but it almost didn't feel real. Then she showed up in the store like a miracle, and I touched her. I kissed her. And it's real and even better than I imagined.

A girl walks out as I reach Hannah's residential building, and she holds the door for me. In front of Hannah's dorm, I rub my palms down my jeans, because I'm sweating, despite the cold. I knock, and within seconds, it flies open under my hand.

It's not Hannah or even Jasmine. It's Sean, Jasmine's Berlin Wall of a boyfriend. He's huge in a way humans aren't supposed to be. And he's scowling at me like I'm something he just scraped off his shoe.

"What do you want?"

"Uh… Is Hannah here?"

Sean glares. "What do you want with her? You gonna lead her on and ditch her again?"

"What? No. That's not—"

"Hold on, hold on." Jasmine inserts herself between Sean and me, laying a hand on his chest. "It's cool. I didn't get a chance to tell you yet, but it's all sorted out. Ben and Hannah are cool."

Sean grunts, and I'm not sure what it means. It doesn't sound like he believes it, or if he does, he isn't very pleased about it. He still looks ready to snap me in half.

"You make her cry again and you'll be sorry."

I wince. "I promise I won't do that again."

"We'll see," he mutters.

"Sean!" Jasmine pushes on his massive chest, backing him into their room. "Relax, okay?"

"Hey, you're here!" I start at Hannah's voice beside me. She's carrying an armload of mail. "Sorry, just checking the mailbox."

"You ready to go?" Because I'm more than ready to get out of Sean's glowering, Hulk-like presence.

"Sure, just let me dump this and grab my coat." She slips past me into her room. I stay out in the hall, where it seems safer. A minute later, she's back, bundled up in a red wool coat with a cream knit beanie on. She looks soft and touchable and really, really cute. I gently tug on a lock of hair. She smiles. "Ready?"

I exhale and cast one last look into her room. "Absolutely."

"Bye, Jasmine. Sean," Hannah calls over her shoulder. "Have fun!"

"I'm watching you, Bookstore Boy!" Sean shouts as we turn to go.

I frown. "Bookstore Boy?"

"Forget it," Hannah mutters, stabbing at the elevator button.

"Is that me?" I grin. "Is that what you call me behind my back?"

The elevator doors open and she sighs. "Shut up. What was that about with Sean?"

"Oh, nothing." We step out of the elevator and start down the hall. "Sean's just letting me know that he'll end me if I screw this up."

Hannah rolls her eyes and laughs. "Yeah, sorry about that."

I hold the door open and usher her outside. "It's okay. I'm pretty sure I had that coming. And I'm really sorry for hurting you like that, Hannah."

She shrugs. "It's not your fault. You just didn't see me the way I saw you."

I shake my head and reach for her hand, then twine our fingers together. "I'm an idiot. Things were happening between us, and I was just too blind and deluded to admit it. You were right to call me out on it."

Hannah hesitates. "So what happened with Alex?" She clears her throat awkwardly, then adds, "Because you've liked her a long time, and you seemed pretty sure—"

"I wasn't. Not really. She seemed like the right choice, but when I met you, I figured out what 'right' really feels like. And it wasn't the same thing at all."

She ducks her chin and smiles, blushing slightly. "Oh."

"I'm sorry I didn't figure it out sooner. I was confused. Conflicted. Whatever. Anyway, I was a total dick to you about her, and I'm really sorry."

"Maybe a little." She smiles. "I was really mad at you that night of the party."

I close my eyes and groan. "As you should have been. Frankly, I'm kinda mad at myself."

She smirks and nudges my shoulder with hers. "Good. Then you can kick your own ass and save me the trouble."

I squeeze her hand. "Deal. For what it's worth, there's nobody in my head but you now."

She smiles, and her whole face lights up. "Then I guess that's all that matters, right?"

"You and me." And right now, that's everything. All the bullshit I left behind at home fades away because I've got Hannah, and she's giving me a chance to do this right.

We cross the bridge over the Tenumbrah River and enter downtown Arlington. Over the weekend, they put up the Christmas decorations. Strings of tiny white lights crisscross over Main Street, and the street lamps are wrapped in evergreen branches. Vendors have set up stalls all along the street, selling candles and jewelry and a bunch of other Christmas gift stuff.

Hannah gasps when she sees it. "It's so pretty."

"Yeah, they set up out here every year. I forgot this is your first year." She tips her head back to look at the lights overhead. They play off her pale skin and make her eyes sparkle. My stomach flips and my heart pounds. How did I ignore what I felt about her for so long?

"Hey, Hannah?"

She turns to look at me, eyes still shining. I reach up and

tuck her hair behind her ear, letting my fingers linger on her neck. "I like you."

That blush I love so much makes an appearance. She laughs softly. "I like you, too."

I step forward until our toes are touching and turn her hand over, until we're palm to palm. "No, I *really* like you. Actually, I'm pretty crazy about you."

"Well, you already know I'm crazy about you. I was shamelessly transparent about it."

"I'm glad you were. If you hadn't told me how you felt, I might have missed this. Thanks for being so brave."

She frowns and shakes her head. "I'm not brave."

"Are you kidding? You're the bravest person I know."

"So are you."

I snort. "Me? Why?"

"It takes guts to stand up to your family. You're following your own path even though they don't approve."

I swallow thickly and look at our joined hands. Right. That. Technically, I never *said* I'd stood up to them, but it feels like lying. Still, nothing's settled yet. I'll figure something out and never have to tell Hannah about the stupid law school application smoldering on my laptop, demanding a decision.

"Yeah, maybe." I start walking again. "So, what are you hungry for?"

If Hannah caught that obvious subject change, she doesn't say so. She falls into step beside me and leans onto my shoulder. It's a perfect night, clear and cold, with the twinkling net of lights overhead and Hannah holding my hand. I want to stop time and live in this moment. The future can stay out there, unlived as far as I'm concerned, because this right here is all I want or need.

Chapter Seventeen

"Your roommate is really dating Sean Jackson?" Dad asks yet again. It's the beginning of winter break. Dad has come to pick me up. Jasmine and Sean left five minutes ago to drive back to Akron, but Dad is still starstruck.

"Yep, since the tenth grade."

"I just wasn't expecting to meet a top NFL prospect in my daughter's dorm room."

"Trust me, when he's with Jasmine, he's just Sean from Akron. I think that's what he likes about her."

"She seems nice."

"She is. We're good friends." I'm going to miss Jasmine over break. And Ben. God, I don't know how I'll manage to go three weeks, even though he's promised to drive to Cleveland at least once to visit. It's not fair. We just got together at the end of Thanksgiving break, three short weeks ago, but we've barely seen each other. He's been buried in the Christmas rush at work and two massive papers due for his classes. I've been studying non-stop for finals, trying to salvage my grades. So far, we've had all of one date, a lot of texts, a few quick cups of coffee between classes, and two make out sessions in the stacks at the library. I think I saw more of him when we were just friends.

And now I'm leaving for break while he stays in Arlington to work. I can't believe it, but I really, *really* don't want to leave.

Of course, that's not only about Ben. I'm terrified to go home.

Finals are over. My chem final went better than I expected, and there's a tiny chance I passed the class. Not that it matters. I'll be out of the Honors Program, and sooner or later, I'll need to stop hiding behind my lies. I'm going to have to tell Dad, and imagining it makes me nauseous. But the hardest thing to tell him will be this: I don't care about the Honors Program anymore.

I'm still toeing the line of expectations and reality. I signed up for half of the recommended chemistry curriculum next semester, the ones I could take even if I get booted from the Honors Program. But on a whim, I added Intro to American Lit and Contemporary Social Justice just because the descriptions in the catalogue sounded amazing. And last week I signed up to volunteer with the Arlington World Outreach Club because some guy handed me a flyer on campus and I got sucked in by the work they do for overseas aid organizations. This is probably not how I should be spending my free time when I'm failing my major.

I don't know what I'm doing anymore. My academic career is a mess, and I'm watching it roll toward the cliff without lifting a finger to stop it. I'm dancing around all these random classes that shouldn't even be on my radar. I'm ignoring the thing I'm supposed to be passionate about because all I really want to do is read.

Telling my dad would be so much easier if I was just shifting focus to another field in science. If I decided I wanted to go to medical school, or work as an immunologist at the CDC. Announcing that my major is going to be "undeclared" feels selfish and like a waste of all my potential.

But I can't stay on the path I started down when I came to Arlington— It feels wrong. I just don't know how to find my way to what feels right.

After securing my dirty laundry basket to the top of my rolling suitcase, Dad looks up and flashes me a warm smile. "Well, your first semester at college is successfully in the bag. Ready to indulge in some holiday merry-making?"

I suppress a grimace. When I turn up with a *D* in Honors Chem, he won't think this semester was so successful. "Sure," I say, with a brightness I don't feel.

He smiles again, this time soft and wistful. "I'm so proud of you, kiddo. Your mom would be, too."

Oh, Jesus, if we don't leave right now, I'm going to start crying. "Thanks, Dad. But we'd better hit the road or else traffic will be a nightmare."

If he notices my red, glassy eyes or the strain in my voice, he never says so.

Chapter Eighteen

BEN

I don't know what I was expecting Hannah's father to be like. She's been beating herself up about disappointing him, which I get, but I guess I imagined someone more imposing like my father, someone with a wrath you don't want to incur. He's not at all like that.

Hannah greets me on the porch of their modest little, white, wood-framed house in the Cleveland suburbs. We have a minute alone to say hello properly, but it's freezing and her dad is waiting, so she tugs my hand and leads me inside.

It's warm and comfortable in her house with nothing remotely flashy— The polar opposite of my parents' house. Hannah looks just like her dad. He's on the short side, and they share light brown hair, which he wears a little long and unkempt. His round, wire-rimmed glasses make him look like a shorter, less gaunt, later-era John Lennon.

When Hannah shyly introduces me to him—she calls me her "friend" and blushes the whole time—he extends his hand and smiles broadly.

"Welcome to Cleveland, Ben. How was your drive? Can I get you a drink? Soda or... Oh, Hannah said you're a senior, so I suppose I should offer you a beer, too, huh?"

He winks at Hannah.

"Dad." She rolls her eyes, but she's smiling, so this must be how they are with each other. He teases her, she pretends to be embarrassed, but she secretly loves it.

"Thanks, but I'm okay," I say. "Thanks for having me, Mr. Gregory."

He waves a hand. "Just Dale is fine. Hannah, why don't you get Ben settled in, and then we go grab some dinner?"

"Sure, where do you want to go?"

"How about Finnegan's?"

Hannah lifts her eyebrows. "Okay. Come on, Ben. The guest bedroom is upstairs."

I follow her up the wood staircase. The wall is lined with framed family photos, with Hannah's face at various ages peering back from most of them. My mother doesn't display family photos in our house. She says it's "low class."

Scattered amongst the pictures are other mementos from Hannah's childhood, every one of them related to science in some way. Certificates from prestigious science camps, state-wide awards, blue ribbons for science fair entries. She's had quite a career already and she's only eighteen. My mother never hung this kind of stuff up, either. Our refrigerator was always fingerprint-free stainless steel, unblemished by a single childish drawing or excellent report card.

"He likes you," she whispers over her shoulder.

"I just got here. How can you tell?"

After she reaches the landing, she turns and grabs the pocket of my hoodie, then tugs me closer. "Because Finnegan's is like *our* place, his and mine."

My eyes widen. "Shit. Do you not want to go there? We can go—"

She laughs. "No, it's great. It's his way of saying, 'Welcome to the family.' Hope that doesn't weird you out too much."

I loop my free arm around her waist. "It's not weird at all. It's actually pretty nice."

She kisses me, but we keep it short and chaste because… Yeah, I'm sure Dale Gregory's hospitality doesn't extend to molesting his daughter on the stairs. Or anywhere else in his house. Dammit.

An hour later and we're tucked into a booth at Finnegan's, sharing a plate of the best chili cheese fries I've ever eaten while Hannah's dad subtly checks me out. My dad would be grandstanding, asserting his own success to make sure that anyone we brought home understood our family's superiority. He'd be asking pointed and rude questions, trying to shake loose a person's weaknesses and ugly secrets.

Dale Gregory just asks me what I'm into. And when we discover a shared love of baseball, the conversation takes a twenty-minute detour into a dissection of our mutual favorite team, the Cleveland Giants. Hannah watches with a bemused exasperation.

"Hannah tells me you're an English major," Dale says when we've bored Hannah with all the sports talk.

And here we go. "Yeah, graduating in June." Out of habit, I brace for subtle and not so subtle digs about my shitty choice of major. After all, he's a scientist, which is a long way from literature. And if my own dad has proven anything, it's that dads have a hard time approving of anything they wouldn't do themselves.

He dunks a fry in a mountain of cheesy chili. "Eliot was always my favorite."

I blink. Eliot? "What?"

"George Eliot. Read them all in college and loved them."

I clear my throat and glance at Hannah, who looks just as surprised as I am. "Eliot's great. I think I've read *Middlemarch* half a dozen times."

He nods. "And you work at a bookstore?" Somehow his questions don't feel like an interrogation. Is he genuinely interested?

"Prometheus Books. It's a used bookstore—"

He breaks into a grin. "I remember Prometheus. Wow, that place has been there since I was at Arlington. Your mother loved that store," he says to Hannah.

She stares. "She did?"

"Sure. I tried telling her that checking out books at the campus library was way easier on her student wallet, but she said there was something romantic about used books. Said they told more than one story."

Hannah swallows and she grips my hand under the table. "Yeah, I get that."

On one hand, I don't know how Hannah could ever be afraid of telling her dad anything. This guy is great. And it's so clear in their every interaction that they adore each other.

But on the other hand, I get her fear of letting people down, even the one not here. Even though she's been gone for eight years, Hannah's mom is always present. And considering how they lost her, how she and Dale joined forces to make sure no one else lost someone that way... Yeah, that's a hell of a thing to turn your back on.

I squeeze her fingers in return. She's got to handle this her own way, but I want her to know I'm here for her however she decides to do it.

Chapter Nineteen

HANNAH

After dinner, I suggest taking a drive through downtown Cleveland, past the Rock and Roll Hall of Fame. It's a pretty transparent attempt to get some time alone, but Dad just smirks and tells us to drive safely.

As I direct Ben through town, we talk about school stuff—Jasmine's trip to Pasadena later this week with Sean while Arlington State plays in the Rose Bowl, poor Ralph stuck actually interacting with customers while Ben is here with me, Ben's roommate, John, doing some kind of mind-blowing research at a satellite array in Arizona over the holidays. We drive past the sports stadiums and Hall of Fame, and I navigate us toward Voinovich Park, where it's quiet and dark this time of night.

I point to a tiny parking lot right off the road. "So you haven't said a word about Christmas with your family."

Ben pulls over and kills the engine. His car always surprises me, nicer and newer than I'd expect for a college student. It's one of those subtle reminders of his family's money that pops up every now and then.

"That's because there wasn't much to tell." Ben runs his thumb along the top of the steering wheel as he stares out the windshield. Cleveland's lights are bright and clear in the cold night air.

I take his hand and weave our fingers together. "No fights?"

"I said as little as humanly possible to avoid one."

"Is your dad still hassling you about law school?"

He smirks and shakes his head sadly. "Steve Fisher never gives up when he knows he's right."

"Ben…" I hesitate. "You wouldn't go, would you? To law school?"

He keeps his face turned toward the view, the glow from the city reflecting off his glasses. "He's not wrong about everything. It would mean a decent paycheck one day."

I frown. Is he…actually considering it? "It would mean you'd be miserable forever."

He shrugs absently. "Who ever said we were guaranteed happiness?"

"You deserve to try to be happy."

"Do I? Sometimes I wonder if I'm just being selfish."

I cross my arms over my chest. "Do you think I'd be selfish if I didn't become a drug researcher like my dad?"

"Of course not. We've talked about this."

"And we've talked about law school, too. Come on, Ben. You know it's not right for you. Quit humoring your dad by pretending to consider it."

"Sorry." He reaches under his glasses to rub his eyes.

"I've just gotten into the habit of agreeing with whatever he says when I go home. It's easier that way."

I smile and squeeze his hand. "Well, cut it out. You're with me now, and I know you better than he does."

He releases my hand and cups my face. "Yeah, you do."

I want to press him further, resolve this once and for all. His diffidence scares me. If he can bend on something so important to him, will he be just as quick to bend when it comes to me?

But I only have him for tonight, for a precious hour alone in his car, and I don't want to waste it poking at him. Besides, I can't imagine what Ben's Christmas must've been like, everybody angry, Ben not speaking, nodding along with everything his jerk father says just to keep the peace.

"I'm sorry," I say. "It sounds like a really terrible Christmas."

He shrugs off his scowl and smiles at me. My stomach flips, just like it did the first time I saw him. "It was. But the day after is shaping up to be pretty terrific."

"I'm really glad you came. Dad likes you."

"I like him, too. He seems great. Not at all an ogre like my dad. He might be a lot more understanding—"

"No." I cut him off as my heart pounds and my hands go cold. "Of course he'll understand. And he'll do his best to hide how horribly disappointed he is. I just…"

"Hey…" Ben takes my face, cradling my cheeks in his palms. "It's okay. You have to deal with it in your own way. But keeping this from him is killing you, Hannah."

"I'll tell him before I go back to school. I just have to figure out how to say it."

"Okay, let's walk through it. You have to tell him you've changed your mind about being a drug researcher."

My heart thuds heavily at the words. "Yeah."

"And you want to major in…"

"That's just it— I have no idea. I'm throwing it away for something I haven't even figured out."

"Well, what do you want to do?"

I curl my hand around his wrist. "Can't we just hide in Prometheus? We'll put the closed sign up, lock the door, camp up in the loft, and spend all day reading. Well, reading and making out."

He makes a sound somewhere between a groan and a chuckle. "That sounds like perfection, but sadly, it's not terribly realistic."

"It's a nice dream, though."

"The best dream."

"We could do half of it."

It's dark in the parking lot, but his teeth glint as he grins. "Which part did you have in mind?"

I lean into him and finally—*finally*—kiss him for real. His mouth opens over mine, our tongues touch, and we both moan slightly as we get what we've wanted for weeks. He keeps it sweet, slow, and gentle at first, but I've missed him so much— I reach for him, sliding my fingers into his hair, tugging him closer to me.

Sitting side-by-side in the car with the center console digging into my ribs isn't going to cut it, so I break the kiss and scramble into his lap. Ben gasps as I straddle his thighs, and when I take his glasses off, his eyes are wide, his expression lust-struck in a way I've never seen before.

I've wanted Ben since the minute I met him, in ways I didn't even understand at the time. Then, after waiting for so long, he was mine, and I still couldn't get more than a few stolen moments with him.

Now we're here, and nobody's around to stop us.

I don't wait for him to make the next move. I lean in and kiss him, sliding my hands around the back of his neck. He's a little slow to kiss me back, and his hands rest tentatively on my hips, but when I stroke his tongue with mine, he finally angles his face to take it deeper. One hand comes up and tangles in my hair as we kiss endlessly.

I inch forward until he's wedged right between my legs. We're both wearing jeans, but it's impossible to miss what this is doing to him. I've never felt this way making out with someone. I always stayed detached before, wondering if I was doing it right, nervous about how far it would go.

Tonight, none of that matters. All I want is Ben, and the way he sets my body on fire. My heart races, and every shift of his fingers sends shocks through my system. I want more of him— I *need* more of him. I roll my hips against his and he groans, low and guttural.

"Hannah," he whispers before kissing me again. I take his hand, still gripping my hip, and slide it up to my breast. He groans again.

"We could get into the backseat," I murmur, kissing down the side of his neck. He squeezes my breast once, like he's not sure he should. I arch into him in encouragement.

"No, we can't."

"Why not?" I nip at his earlobe, and his head falls back onto the headrest.

"Hannah, somebody could see."

I start to tell him he's being ridiculous, but then a car passes us in the parking lot, its headlights briefly illuminating us, as if to underscore his point.

I sigh and slump against him. "Okay, maybe you're right."

He chuckles, kisses my temple, and runs his fingers through my hair and down my back. I probably should climb off his lap. Grinding on him isn't helping to dial this back.

He hisses slightly as I slide off him and back into the passenger seat. Then he sits still for a second with his eyes closed, trying to will away his erection, I guess. And maybe we're not doing it tonight in the cold backseat of his car on the side of the highway, but we're doing it soon.

After a couple minutes, he restarts the car. "Come on. Your dad seems to like me so far. I don't want to blow it by bringing you home past curfew."

I laugh. "Are you kidding? I'm way too responsible to have ever needed a curfew. But yeah, if you don't want me to drag you into the backseat, we'd better get out of here."

He closes his eyes and sighs. "Stop tempting me."

"Stop being so temping."

He smirks. "Nobody's ever called me 'tempting' before."

I lean in and kiss his cheek, lingering for just a second, letting the heat simmer between us. "You know I can't get enough of your big…brain."

We erupt into laughter, because let's be real, I'm a little ridiculous as a seductress. The laughter dispels the last of the tension and the heavy conversation that came before. Our futures are still hanging there, like black clouds over our heads. But all I want to think about is what we were doing five minutes ago in the driver's seat. And what else we might do when we finally get back to Arlington and can get some time alone.

I've never been so excited for Christmas break to be over.

Chapter Twenty

"Did you even hear what I read?" Hannah arches an eyebrow at me. She came over hours ago. We ordered pizza and ate it while laughing at terrible reality shows, but now we're wedged together on the couch, Hannah on her back and me on my side.

I'm more on her than off, with my head on her chest and my leg thrown across hers while she reads *Fear and Loathing in Las Vegas* aloud and lazily strokes her fingers through my hair. I might pass out from pleasure.

"Of course I heard. He took drugs and did something crazy."

"The whole book's about that."

My hand is resting on her stomach, rubbing back and forth. Her hoodie—well, *my* hoodie—has ridden up a little. She stole it right before winter break, and while I miss it, I don't miss it as much as I like seeing her wear it. Every time my fingers brush the bare skin beneath her belly button, her voice wobbles. It's been fun seeing how long she's going to keep diligently working through the book until she cracks.

We started reading *Fear and Loathing* right after winter break two weeks ago, but we're still not very far into it. Mostly because reading starts like this—lying together on my couch or her bed—and ends with us wrapped around each other and the book forgotten on the floor.

Hannah's voice is hypnotic as she picks up where she left off reading. Out in the world when she's speaking, she sounds like any ordinary girl. But when we're together like this and she's reading, she slips into this sleepy lower register that I can't resist. I can't believe I never noticed it before we were "us." Or maybe I only hear her like this because we *are* "us."

My hand sweeps across her stomach again, and my fingertips skim the waistband of her jeans. She shudders.

"Do you want me to stop reading?" she says haughtily.

I chuckle. "No, keep going. I'm enjoying this." Damn, am I ever.

She might still be reading *Fear and Loathing*, or she might be reciting the periodic table for all I know. I kiss her just above the edge of her shirt, underneath her collarbone.

Fear and Loathing topples to the floor beside us. Her freed hand joins the other in my hair, and she hauls my head up until she can kiss me. Her mouth is hot, and she must've been thinking about this kiss for a while because she devours me, her tongue slipping into my mouth to find mine. She tastes so good—soft, sweet, and warm—and her smooth curves pressed against me feels even better. I slide my hand up under the hoodie, and she shifts to let me. Then she hooks her leg around my hips, and I'm *right there*.

I groan into her mouth. Fuck, I'm so hard already. I want her so badly. I grind against her, and her moan sends a jolt straight into my dick. I want so much more than this, but I won't rush things, not with Hannah. It's been a long time since I've been with someone, and I'm desperate for her, but her first time wasn't going to happen with her drunk at that party, not in the backseat of my car on the side of the road. And it most definitely isn't going to happen in the middle of a make out session on the couch, no matter how eager we are. Even though it's the very last thing I want to do, I shift my weight off her and slow my kisses down, just soft and closed-mouth.

Hannah tugs on my shoulders, but I stay where I am, beside her. Abruptly, she leans back and opens her eyes.

"What's wrong?"

I blink at her. "What do you mean?"

"Why did you stop?"

"We didn't stop. We haven't stopped."

She narrows her eyes at me. "Ben, you know what I mean. What's going on?"

"I, um, I just don't want you to think—"

"You know I'm not a virgin, right?"

Wait, what? *Holy shit.* "No," I say, strangled as the possibilities flit behind my eyes and make my dick twitch. "I didn't."

Hannah scoffs. "You just assumed because what? I look innocent?"

She's right, of course. You'd think I'd have learned by now never to assume I have her figured out. She's not a virgin. Shit, *she's not a virgin.* "I thought…you seemed…"

"I think I seemed pretty eager. Because I *am* pretty eager."

I gulp so hard it's audible. "You are?"

Her frown disappears, and a smile teases around the corners of her mouth. She slides one palm slowly up the back of my neck and threads her fingers into my hair. My whole spine shudders. "You can't tell?"

And damn, it's that voice again, that low, sultry, reading-out-loud voice. "Yeah, but I didn't want to rush you."

She leans up until her mouth is an inch from mine. "You're not rushing me, Ben. In fact, I'm about to climb on top of you and take matters into my own hands."

Okay. We're done here. I slam my mouth down on hers and roll onto her. She moans, a soft, sensual sound that'll be the fucking end of me. I shift between her legs again, and her heels hook over my thighs. I push her hoodie up— I want it off. Her shirt and the bra, too. I don't even care where we are anymore. If she wants it, I'm there. We'll do it on the couch, on the floor, any flat surface that holds still for us.

I can't get her clothes off without breaking the kiss, but I get her shirt up and her bra unhooked. I slide my hand under the silky fabric and cup her breast— And my phone vibrates on the coffee table. I collapse onto her, groaning into her hair. She laughs.

I grope one-handed to the side for my stupid, fucking phone. "I'll just put it on silent."

She starts wiggling out from under me. "You might as well answer now. The moment's gone." She leans forward, grabs my phone, and holds it out to me, frowning. "It's a Chicago number."

My stomach bottoms out— It can only be one person.

Richard Parker's been emailing me since Thanksgiving about the law program at the Chicago College of Law, and if he's calling me now, it can't be good.

Because I sent the application in.

It was Christmas Day, and Dad wouldn't shut up about it, so I just did it, half-assed, daring them to reject me. That's not how this game is played, though, because Dad's got an in and that in is now calling me. There's so much inappropriate nepotism happening here that I feel ill, but this is the way it works in Dad's world. It's all about who you know, who can do you a favor, who can give you a leg up.

I glance at Hannah before pressing accept as I stand up and turn away.

"Hello?"

"Ben? It's Richard Parker."

My heart sinks. Why did I even answer?

"Hi, Richard. What's up?"

"I've got some great news. I'm calling in an unofficial capacity here, but I wanted you to know that the admissions committee has accepted you. Congratulations and welcome to the Chicago College of Law!"

I swallow hard. Some rapidly shrinking part of my mind is horrified. But the rest is just…blank. I'm too stunned to feel anything.

Richard keeps talking to fill the awkward silence. "Your personal statement was a little weaker than some applicants, but that was made up for by your excellent LSAT scores."

My personal statement sucked because I wrote it in twenty minutes on Christmas Day. The fact that they took it seriously makes a mockery of this process. And I took the LSATs last spring to get my dad off my back when he first started cracking down about my major. I figured I'd bomb it, thereby displaying my lack of law aptitude, but I aced it. Unfortunately. So here I am, doing my best to fail at this and somehow not.

Six months ago, law school in Chicago seemed as likely to me as studying marine biology in Beijing, but now it's looking terrifyingly likely. I glance at Hannah, sitting on the couch, one leg folded up under her, watching as I pace around the room. I haven't said anything specific, but she's not dumb. She knows something's up.

"That's um…thank you," I mutter.

"Like I said, this is just an unofficial call. You'll get an official offer in the mail in the next day or so. Make sure you sign and return it right away. There's a long wait list, so they need to lock in the incoming class as soon as possible."

"Sure thing. Thanks, Richard."

"No problem, Ben. Say hi to your dad for me."

"Will do." I haven't spoken to him since Christmas, and I've ignored every harassing text he's sent me.

I end the call and stare at my phone. What the hell am I going to do?

"What was that about?" Hannah asks.

I don't want to burden her with my shit. We're still in this vague phase where we're able to have fun without knowing where this is going or feeling like it has to *go* anywhere. So I keep my response offhand. "Just this friend of my dad's. He's still hassling me about law school."

She sighs and shakes her head. "When are you going to tell him about grad school?"

"I don't know. It's complicated. He's making things difficult."

"If you just talk to him—"

"I can't, Hannah. You *know* why I can't." My voice is sharper than I intended, and she draws back a little. I drop down onto the couch and pull her into my arms. "Sorry. I'm sorry. I didn't mean to snap at you. It's just—I mean, you get it. You haven't told your dad, either."

She lays her head on my shoulder. "And we both know I'm being a total baby about that."

Despite the anxiety making me nauseous, I chuckle. "Is that your way of calling me a baby?"

She giggles, but after a moment, she lifts her head and looks me in the eye. "No, it's my way of saying we should man up together."

I stroke a hand up her thigh. "That's a new word for it."

She slaps at my chest. "I'm serious. Maybe I won't be so freaked out about talking to my dad if I know you're doing something just as scary at the same time. Like in *Titanic*. 'You jump, I jump.'"

I roll my eyes. "You did not just quote *Titanic* to me."

"Yes, I did. Shut up, you big snob. So?"

"So you want us to sign a pact or something?"

"No, we just go and do it. This weekend. Get it over with, like ripping off a Band-Aid."

There's something appealing about her idea. The thought of Hannah dealing with her dad while I'm dealing with mine… Weirdly, her bravery makes me brave. I don't even know what the repercussions of my actions will be, but it's about time I found out. I can't keep living in this limbo, trying to keep all the balls in the air, knowing at some point I'll have to let one drop.

"Okay, let's do it. We'll both go home and face the

music."

Hannah swallows, worry clouding her eyes. For all her bravery, she's not fearless, but she still says, "Deal."

We haven't done anything yet, and who the hell knows what'll happen when we do? But just deciding to act makes me feel lighter than I have in months. Like I have the power to shape my future.

I gently lift her chin. "It'll be okay."

"I know. I feel better knowing I'm doing it with you."

I smile and run my knuckle down the curve of her cheek. "Same."

She hooks her hands behind my neck and leans in, until she's so close I can feel her breath on my lips. "So... That thing we were discussing earlier? Is it too late to recapture that moment?"

"Actually, I kind of feel like celebrating right now. Is that weird?"

"If your idea of celebrating involves lots of kissing and not a lot of clothes, I'm totally on board."

Chapter Twenty-One

HANNAH

We kiss for a while on the couch until I'm straddling his lap and his hands are under my shirt again. It's like when we were in his car in Cleveland— Except we're not in a car. And we're alone.

Ben kisses under my jaw and down my neck. "Do you..." He clears his throat and his words vibrate across the sensitive skin of my neck. "Do you want to move to the bedroom?"

My stomach clenches with a combination of nerves and anticipation. Mostly anticipation. I slide back off his lap and take his hand, smiling at him. His dark eyes are half closed, and he smiles back at me, then kisses my fingertips. For all the intense making out and grinding, the feather-light kisses on the pads of my fingers make me melt.

When he stands, he curls his free hand around the back

of my neck and kisses me again, a long, slow exploration of my mouth that catches fire. I dig my fingers into his hair, holding him tight to me, and he wraps an arm around my back before pulling me up onto the tips of my toes. God, I love how tall he is. When we're together like this, it's like he enfolds me.

We stumble toward his room, Ben walking backward, unable to stop kissing long enough to get there properly. He backs into a table, nearly sending his laptop to the floor, but he catches it, and then we laugh, all the nerves and excitement making us a little giddy.

After saving his laptop, Ben keeps backing into his room, tugging me by my hands, but not kissing this time, so we don't run into anything else. Which works until he trips over a pile of laundry on the floor just inside his room.

Ben's room is a mess. Not in a gross way, but he doesn't put his clothes away in the closet or the dresser. There are piles on the floor, some clean, some dirty, and he sorts it out that way. The bed is perpetually unmade. There are books piled everywhere. I keep one book on my nightstand— Ben has nine, and another pile on the floor next to the bed. His bookshelf is stacked two-deep, and more sit on the floor in front of it. But aside from that, he doesn't own much. Despite his family's money, there isn't a fancy stereo or electronic gadget. Just whatever he needs to live and books.

"Maybe we should sit." I skirt around him and the clothes, shrugging out of his hoodie as I go, and perch onto the edge of his bed. His eyes take me in, sitting here, waiting for him, and the look on his face— I flush hot and cold all over.

"Come here," I whisper.

Ben sits and angles into me, one hand braced on the bed behind me, the other dragging a knuckle along my jaw.

"Hey," he murmurs.

I trace his lips with my fingertip. "Hey, yourself."

"We don't have to—"

I press my finger against his lips. "I want to."

I take his glasses off and lean past him to set them onto the stack of books beside the bed. When I straighten up, his eyes are different—darker and intense—and his lips are slightly parted.

He takes my face in his hands and pulls me into his kiss. No gentleness this time. This kiss is hungry, hot, and a little desperate. He nips at my bottom lip and I moan. Then he leans into me, pressing me back onto the bed. He rolls, and I'm under him, his knee between my thighs, and I ache as I press against him. I've never wanted anything as much as I want Ben right now.

I'm lost—in kisses that last forever and his hands tracing my face, my neck, and shoulder, waist, and hip. I'm lost in the weight of his body pressing me into the mattress, his leg tight against me, winding me up to greater and greater heights. I'm lost in the sounds we're making, the deep labored breaths, quiet sighs, and tiny moans every time one of us touches someplace new.

"Hannah…" He kisses the side of my neck, his lips pulling on my skin and making me weak in the knees. I fist the back of his T-shirt, and his hand shifts to my waist, under my shirt where his fingers spread over my ribcage.

"Are you sure?" he mutters into my skin.

I pull back enough to look at him, and I hold his face, so he looks at me. "Shut up and stop worrying."

He grins and kisses me again. The air shifts around us as this moves from a serious make out session to real foreplay. This time when I fist my hand in his hair, his hips flex into mine, and his hardness presses against me, making me moan.

Slowly, he works my shirt up until he can't get it higher without breaking our kiss. He leans back and looks into my face, his dark eyes full of emotion as he watches me. His Adam's apple bobs and he's still hesitating, still afraid of rushing me, which is sweet but unnecessary. I grab the hem of my shirt and strip it over my head. His eyes fall immediately to my bra. I never thought my breasts were all that much to shout about, but Ben's looking at them like he wants to worship at their altar. It makes me feel sexy and brave, so I arch my back and unhook the clasp of my bra.

His eyes flash briefly to mine, and I smile, so he draws the straps slowly down my arms. When I'm naked from the waist up, he just looks at me again, and not just at my breasts. His gaze skates over my face, my arms, my chest, and then his hand follows the same path, cupping my cheek, tracing a line down the side of my neck, over my shoulder until his palm lands on my breast.

He drags in a shaky breath. I've stopped breathing altogether.

"You're so beautiful," he whispers and kisses me again. I melt as he kisses and touches me. Then he dips his head and draws my nipple into his mouth. I gasp and try desperately to hold still under him, but it feels incredible. I'm on fire, all tingling nerves and tense muscles. His soft hair brushes against my chest, a different sensation than his mouth, but no less powerful. He runs his hands along the length of me, from my knee, to my thigh, over my hip, along my rib cage, and up to cup my breast, holding it still as his mouth works its magic.

I need so much more than this. Tugging at his shirt, I make him pause long enough to strip it off, and then we're bare chest to bare chest. His skin is so smooth, so warm, and he slides one hand between my shoulder blades. He holds me like I'm precious. Like he'll never let go.

I slip my hand between us to unbutton his jeans. He drops his head into the crook of my neck, breathing heavily as I drag the zipper down, brushing against him as I do.

"I'll die if you touch me right now," he mutters.

"Should I stop?" I tease, arching an eyebrow when he lifts his head to look at me. His hair is a tousled mess, and he's grinning adorably.

"Maybe just wait until I can touch you, too."

Then he rears off me, stands by the bed, grasps my jeans at the hem, and tugs them off. There's no way it's not awkward, even with both of us working together, but despite the laughter, he frees me from my jeans. His go next and they're a lot easier. Then he's standing by the bed in just his boxers, his hand on my knee, his eyes on mine. With the soft light from his bedside lamp illuminating his body, long, lean, and lightly muscled, he's beautiful.

When he lowers himself back down on top of me, all traces of humor are gone. He looks serious, almost reverent. I lift my knees, allowing him to settle between my legs, and we kiss—long, slow, deep kisses, rocking into each other as we do. There's just my underwear and his boxers between us, and they're not doing anything to keep his hard ridge from pressing against me. Each shift of our bodies creates an addictive friction. Everything is warm and heavy.

This is already the best sex I've ever had, and we're not even *having* it yet. Except it feels like we are, like this is more than just a collection of body parts slotting together. It feels so much bigger because I love him.

He brushes my hair out of my face as he presses slow, soft kisses to my lips, my cheeks, my chin. "I love you, Hannah," he whispers, and my heart feels like it's expanding, too full of emotion. My eyes water. I pull his face back to mine and pour everything I'm feeling into my kiss.

"I love you, too."

Ben's hand moves to my thigh and slowly strokes up and down. His fingers curl around the back of my knee to pull it up. He settles more firmly against me and moans quietly. When his fingers come back up and brush against the edge of my underwear, he looks me in the eye and raises his eyebrows in question. I nod, and he hooks his finger onto the side of my underwear and tugs them down. I take over, getting them all the way off while he deals with his boxers. He leans away to the bedside table to grab a condom.

When he comes back to me, he runs his hand down my face again, tracing my lips and down over my chin to my neck.

"I do love you," he says. "So much. No matter what happens." He kisses me again as his body settles over mine. I lace my fingers behind his neck and pull him down until our lips are brushing together.

"I love you, too," I whisper, the repeated words like an incantation, more real every time we say them.

He pushes into me and gasps my name. The pressure of him filling me takes me by surprise— He's bigger than I expected. But it feels good, overwhelmingly good, and I sigh as he pushes deep inside. When he moves, the rhythm shocks me— I don't remember it ever feeling like this. The handful of other times, it was like following instructions in a kit—step one, step two—just to get to the finished product, which never really happened for me anyway. But with Ben, it's entirely different. Every move we make together feels instinctual. Every time he touches me, I respond on some elemental level. It's like my body isn't even my own anymore.

He kisses my shoulder, his lips pressing against my sweaty skin. He's breathing heavily as he whispers, "God, you feel so…"

"I know." I fist one hand into his hair and wrap my other arm around his back. "You, too."

I cling to his shoulders and bury my face in his neck, kissing his skin, tasting the salt of his sweat on my lips. I'm overwhelmed with sensation, with the building tension. Just when I can't bear it anymore, Ben shifts and something ignites deep inside of me, a slow-motion detonation that ends in a blinding flash of pleasure. He kisses me, swallowing my cries as I fall apart in his arms, and his pace increases. He's holding me so tight. I'm wrapped in the cocoon of his body. Then Ben gasps and buries his face in my neck as he comes.

Neither of us makes any effort to move. I couldn't if I tried. I don't want to. I want to lie here under Ben, in his arms, for the rest of my life. Sublime happiness like I've never known burns under my skin. I drag one hand up and down his back while I run the fingers of my other hand through his hair. Ben groans and presses a kiss to my shoulder, and we float together a while longer.

After he cleans up and lies beside me again, he pulls me into his side, my head on his shoulder, his arm around me.

Our free hands are joined, fingers tightly intertwined on his chest.

"This was…" He pauses, searching for the right words. "I've never felt like this."

I smile and bury my face in his shoulder. "Me, neither."

"Thank you for loving me. Please don't stop."

I love Ben and he loves me. But he also *needs* me. It sets off something warm and protective in me. No one's ever needed me like this before. This is more than infatuation or physical chemistry. This is *alchemy*, which I didn't think was real until tonight. Chemistry is predictable. If you understand the elements, you know how they'll combine and what they'll produce. Alchemy implies magic, the elements combining to become something more than the sum of their parts, lead transforming into gold. And I didn't think magic existed in the real world, but maybe it does — a certain kind of magic. Because this is what it feels like when your life changes, when base metal becomes gold.

Chapter Twenty-Two

HANNAH

Now that Ben and I have taken this major step, all I want to do is stay in bed with him. Everything was so perfect—not just the sex, although that part was *great*—but the touching and words and I love yous felt amazing. Leaving his side even for a minute is hard, but we promised we'd do this. You jump; I jump.

So I take the bus back to Cleveland first thing Saturday morning. It's two hours by car but four by bus with all the stops, so it's noon before I get home. Dad's not there. I'm not surprised. When he's deep into the critical stages of a project, he often works on the weekends to obsess over data.

I'll go crazy sitting around the house, waiting for him to get home— Mom's face looks at me from a dozen pictures, compounding my guilt. So I take the city bus out to the Park Pharmaceuticals facility to see him, like I've done since I was old enough to ride the bus alone.

The Park building is quiet on a Saturday. There are a handful of people working because they're on a deadline, or the experiment is too critical to be left for the weekend, or they're obsessed workaholics like my dad. The empty labs I pass are familiar and weirdly comforting. Other girls went to Girl Scouts; I hung out at Park and mixed simple compounds while my dad worked. I practically grew up in this place.

I find him alone in his lab, of course. He's got three computer displays across his desk, all lit up with rows and rows of complex data. Next to that is an array of glass beakers in metal holders and several trays of samples. The sight is so familiar, so comforting, that my throat closes up. I wish I could undo whatever's happened inside of me. I wish I could love it as much as he does. Our whole relationship has developed in labs like this. If I walk away, what will come next?

The door thumps closed behind me, and Dad glances up. His eyes light up behind his glasses.

"Surprise," I say, with a weak wave.

"Hannah! What are you doing here? Is everything okay?"

"Yeah, everything's fine. I just thought I'd come home for the weekend and surprise you. Is that okay?"

He hesitates for just a second, his eyes flicking over me, like he can sense my distress. But he smiles and says, "Of course it is. You know you can come home whenever you want."

"Can you leave long enough to get lunch?" I gesture at whatever he's working on.

He sighs and glares at the glass beakers. "Yes, it's fine. I was about to call it quits on this round anyway. I'll start fresh this afternoon. Just give me a minute to shut down, and we'll go to Finnegan's. Sound good?"

"Chili cheese fries always sound good."

He goes to work breaking down the experiment while I wander around, looking at the other tables in the lab.

"You know, that was your mother's station," he says, when I pause at one. He's told me that almost every time I come. It was like she was here with us, watching us work together. Watching me work toward a noble future I don't want anymore. My neck goes hot, and my stomach twists. God, I'm so selfish, and the longer I stay here, the harder it is to keep it in. The truth is just behind my lips— I can't wait until Finnegan's. I have to get it out now or I never will.

"Dad, I failed my first chemistry test." It comes out in a rush, a panicked exhale.

Dad faces me. "What?"

My voice cracks when I speak— Am I crying? "I failed my first chem test. I thought I knew everything on it, but I just blanked. Dad, I flunked chemistry. *Chemistry!* And now I'm out of the Honors Program, and there's no way I can salvage it." I gasp for air, but I can't stop this stream of words. They're fighting their way up my throat, pushed out by Liesel Meminger, Owen Meany, and Sam Clay.

"Hannah," Dad says softly as he skirts a table to get to me. "What is it, sweetheart? What's going on?"

I knew he wouldn't be mad— I could have handled anger. It's the disappointment that breaks me.

A wave of sobs breaks free and I double over, wrapping my arms around myself, trying to hold together even though I seem determined to fall apart. "I'm so sorry, Dad. I don't know what happened. As soon as I was away at college doing it on my own, I realized…" Can I say it? I don't want to— He's going to be so disappointed. I'm throwing it away, everything we built together, all those years of preparation. The dreams we shared and the nights right here in this lab— I'm walking away.

"Realized what, Hannah?" He holds my shoulders. "Come on, sweetie. You're scaring me."

I take huge, gasping gulps of air until I can calm the sobs enough to speak. "All these years, me doing chemistry…"

"Yeah?"

"I think it was really about *us* doing chemistry. I loved it because it was our thing, not because I loved it for myself. You love it for Mom's sake, and I wanted to do it for her, too."

Dad exhales slowly. I close my eyes so I don't have to see the disappointment there. "I'm so sorry, Dad."

"Hannah," he says, his voice shaky. "Sweetie, look at me."

I open my burning, teary eyes and meet his. They're teary, too— God, how could I do this to him?

"Honey, if I've pushed you too hard—"

"No! I wanted it, too. I wanted to be just like you and work in a lab and develop drugs and save lives. I'm just… I'm not sure I do anymore." I barely get out the last word before I dissolve into sobs again. Dad pulls me into his chest and shushes me, stroking my hair and making nonsense noises the way he did when I had nightmares as a little girl.

"Hannah, listen to me. I never wanted you to follow in my footsteps— I want you to be *happy*. Your mother would have wanted you to be happy. If there's something else you want to do—"

"That's just it. I have *no idea* what I want to do. I just know this doesn't feel right anymore. And I'm reading all these books, and there's so much stuff I don't know anything about, and I don't know what to do anymore."

"Hey." He takes half a step back so he can look me in the eye again. "You're eighteen, Hannah. You don't have to know. You seemed so set on chemistry, and I was happy to guide you, if that's what you wanted. But it's okay to want something different."

I sniff a big, wet, ungraceful snort. "Really?"

"Really. Want to know a secret?"

"What?"

"Your mother changed majors three times before she declared for chem."

My mouth drops open. "But you said you guys met in class."

"We did, when she finally decided this was what she wanted. We got to know each other because I was tutoring her to get her up to speed after her late start. It's okay to not know what you want right now, and it's okay to change your mind, and change it again. You're smart and you've got so much heart. You'll know it when the right thing finds you."

His words feel like oxygen after staying underwater too long. I cling to every one like a lifeline. "I was so afraid of telling you. I was supposed to do it for Mom's sake, just like you. I thought you'd be disappointed."

He winces. "I'm so, so sorry if I made you feel that way. You never owed your mother or me anything, Hannah. This is your life."

"You didn't." I start blubbering again, but it's okay because so is Dad. He hugs me and I cry on his shoulder like I've wanted to all year. And he says everything's going to be okay, just like he's always done. I don't know why I believed for a second he wouldn't.

Chapter Twenty-Three

BEN

I'm pretty sure my dad knows something's up the minute I turn up for a surprise visit early Saturday afternoon. I quit coming home for weekends halfway through freshman year and don't show my face unless commanded to do so, but I promised Hannah, so here I am.

We make it through a hideously awkward dinner in one piece. I almost wish Gav was here because at least he breaks the tension, usually by saying something stupid. But it's just me and Dad, and I have to do this.

Hannah's in Cleveland to see her dad, but there's no way Dale will blow up at her the way my dad will blow up at me. But it's not about what Dale does, it never has been. It's about what's in her head, and I know this is hard for her. But if she can do it, so can I.

Mom chatters on about the bitchy thing some lady at

her gym did while she sips her wine and doesn't eat, and Dad talks about the Bengals game last Saturday. Finally, Mom says she's full—after barely breathing on her food—and excuses herself to make a phone call. Dad gets up to refill his whiskey from the bar against the dining room wall.

I wish I hadn't eaten because I feel sick. But it's now or never. Hannah's handling it right now and so can I.

"Hey, Dad, I need to talk to you about something."

He glances over his shoulder at me with an arched eyebrow— I've never willingly come to talk to him about anything before. But he replaces the stopper on the decanter and casually says, "Shoot." Like we do this all the time.

"It's about law school."

His shoulders stiffen, and he straightens his spine. He's already pissed off, and I haven't even said anything.

"I take it you heard from Richard?"

I shouldn't be surprised he already knows I made it in. Hell, Richard probably called him before he called me. It's disgusting. If I were going to law school, I'd at least want to get in honestly, because I deserved it. Not like this, as some favor between college buddies. That little flare of anger gives me the fuel I need to keep going.

"I did. And while I appreciate Richard's help, I can't go to law school."

Dad turns from the bar to face me. "Can't?" he says quietly. Too quiet. There's a dangerous energy about him that I hate.

"Won't. It's not what I want to do with my life, and I can't keep pretending it is."

"It's not what you want to do," he echoes back, still in that eerily quiet voice.

I swallow thickly and soldier on. I'm into it now. No going back. "No. Look, the head of the English Department at Arlington says I'm the best student he's had in years. He wants me to stay on and get my master's under him, and that—"

He doesn't let me finish— His nostrils flare and eyes narrow as his rage boils over. His whiskey sloshes precipitously in his glass. "Listen, sport. The time for goofing around is over."

I want to tell him that the work I've done for the past four years hardly counts as goofing around, but he won't care. The things I've done that I'm proud of mean nothing to him.

"I'm not letting you waste any more time on a major that'll leave you strapped for cash."

"Dad, it's not—"

"Ben, I'm gonna be straight." He fixes me with his pale blue eyes, his thick blond eyebrows furrowed together over his nose. "If you don't get your ass to law school next fall, you're on your own. No money for school, no money for anything, the trust fund goes, and not a dime from this family ever again. Are we clear?"

My heart stops. Dad's never approved of my major; I've always caught grief about it. But he's never threatened to fucking cut me off. He's talking about disowning me, and he absolutely means it. If I don't go to law school, I'm penniless. My shitty salary from Prometheus won't even cover my rent, never mind anything else.

He sips his whiskey calmly, watching me mull it over. I've read about people facing crossroads in their life, but I never thought I'd face one so stark myself. I could tell him to shove it and walk away, but what if I can't make grad school happen on my own? Then I've blown my family apart for nothing, and I end up writing ad copy or something just as unfulfilling.

Or I could agree. I won't be happy, but I'll survive. I told Hannah over Christmas break that none of us are guaranteed happiness. Maybe it all comes down to that. What I've been doing up until now was a kid's fantasy, but now it's time to grow up.

Dad takes another sip of his drink. "So what's it gonna be?"

I'm staring at the yawning black cavern of my future if I turn my back on this, and I don't know if I have what it takes to get to the other side on my own.

"Ben, you're a smart kid. You know what to do here," he says, like he only wants what's best for me. And maybe he does in his own twisted way. It's about control with my dad, but it's also about picking the right future, and that's a no-brainer for him. Maybe it should be for me, too.

"Yeah, I guess I do," I finally mutter.

"So you're sending back that acceptance letter as soon as it shows up? Right?"

The acceptance letter arrived the day after Richard called. All I have to do is sign.

I swallow thickly and nod. "Right."

Chapter Twenty-Four

HANNAH

I lose track of time for the rest of the day. I went home with Dad, and we had a long talk about what my first semester at college was really like. I told him everything—bombing the first test, the anxiety and fear, discovering Prometheus and the books that Ben gave me, all the things those books made me think and feel...

It's a long day, ultimately good, but really draining. By the time I climb the stairs to my room, I'm exhausted, but I need to call Ben. He was facing something just as daunting today, and I'm sure it was worse for him because I'd bet his dad wasn't nearly as supportive as mine.

I call him after climbing into bed, but it goes straight to voicemail. That gives me a flicker of unease, but I'm being ridiculous. There are a million perfectly harmless reasons Ben might not be able to pick up his phone. I really wanted to talk to him tonight, but it can wait until morning.

I fire off a quick text before I go to sleep.

Dad was great. Everything is okay. How did it go with you? Miss you.

He hasn't texted back by morning, which is more worrying. But based on everything he's told me, it's possible his dad is still trying to force his hand.

I text him again to say Dad's driving me back to Arlington, and I'll be there by early afternoon. I can't imagine Ben will stay in Columbus any longer than absolutely necessary, so I'll just head over to his apartment as soon as I get back. I'm desperate to hear how it went and tell him about my talk with Dad, but it's probably better to have that conversation face-to-face anyway.

Weirdly, as hard as yesterday was, I feel great. The fear and dread I've been dragging around with me for months is gone, and I'm free. I'm still completely directionless, but my future will sort itself out, and Dad will be there for me no matter what.

Now my only concern is Ben. By mid-afternoon, I still haven't received a single phone call or text, so I head over to his place. It's Sunday, so he's got to be back— He has classes and work tomorrow.

Ben and his friend, John, live in this ramshackle Victorian house in the student ghetto. It was a nice house once, but it was split up into quirky little apartments decades ago and has had generations of Arlington students living there ever since. Putting it kindly, it's a mess of sloping floors, drafty windows, and sticking doors.

I ring the bell and bounce on my toes on the sagging front porch, trying to stay warm. A second later, the door opens, but it's not Ben.

"Oh." John smiles. "Sorry, I must have been already coming downstairs when you buzzed."

"Is Ben back?"

"Yeah, he just got in a little while ago. I think he's in the shower."

"Oh, should I come back?"

John grins and waves me in. "Just go up. He won't care."

John heads out, and I climb the two flights of stairs to their tiny apartment. It's kind of cute because it's up in the old attic, so it has angled ceilings and weird little poky corners. The shower is still running as I pass the bathroom, and the thought of Ben in there, under the water, makes me pause.

What would he do if I joined him there? My pulse races, but yeah... I'm not brave enough to go for that just yet. But maybe someday soon.

Ben's room, as usual, looks like a closet and a bookshelf got in a fight and nobody won. His backpack has practically exploded across his unmade bed, and I'm kinda hoping we'll need that bed later.

When I toss his clothes from the bed into a pile and straighten the books and papers into a tidy stack, a letter printed on creamy, heavy paper with an embossed school logo at the top of the stack catches my eye. It's the logo for the Chicago College of Law.

I shouldn't read it, but the first word jumps off the paper at me: *Congratulations*.

I can't help it— I keep reading. *"Congratulations on*

your acceptance to the Chicago College of Law."

The middle stuff I don't care about, but it closes with, *"Please sign and return this letter as soon as possible to secure your place in the incoming class."*

And below that, unmistakably, is Ben's signature.

Ben walks into the room in sweats and a T-shirt, rubbing a towel over his wet hair, but he drops the towel when he sees me. "Hey, what are you doing here?"

I clear my throat. "I came to see how you were because I was worried. Seems I didn't need to be. You've got everything all figured out."

His gaze drops to the paper in my shaking hand, and his expression goes flat. Not shocked or nervous, just resigned.

"What the hell is this, Ben?"

He sighs, loud and frustrated. I move toward him, letter in hand.

"I was going to talk to you when you got back—"

"You've been telling me over and over that you won't go, but you've been planning it this whole time."

"No—"

"Yes, you were! When did you apply?"

He looks away, his jaw working as he grinds his teeth together. "Christmas day. I just did it to shut my dad up."

I wave the letter. "Did you just accept the spot to shut him up, too? Are you going to spend three years getting a degree just to shut him up?"

Ben sighs. "It's complicated."

"Yeah, you keep saying that, but it seems pretty straight-forward to me. Your dad is telling you what to do, and you're doing it."

"You don't understand." He's not meeting my eyes, and

those words are so dismissive. The room goes hot— I clench my fists. After everything we've been through, we're right back here, with Ben discounting me, underestimating me.

"Then explain it to me! You know what you want, and Ben, this isn't it."

"I don't have a choice!"

"You always have a choice."

Ben barks a humorless laugh and spins away, hooking his hands behind his neck. "I don't. If I don't do this, I lose everything. This is bigger than a major, Hannah— I'm talking about the rest of my life, here. You don't get it."

I reel back. "I don't *get it*? Seriously? I've been working toward my major since I was four. I was supposed to major in chem and become a drug researcher and cure the fucking disease that killed my *mom*. I was working for a lot more than just some major, and I walked away from that. And you think I don't *get it*— What, because I'm some dumb *freshman*? I just went home and told my dad everything. You went home and caved. Tell me who the grown up is here."

His eyes glint behind his glasses, and his eyebrows furrow into an angry line. "It's not the same thing at all," he snaps. "We're in entirely different situations. Yeah, you quit the Honors Program, but you still have your dad. Whatever you fucking deal with, he loves you, and he'll always support you. I don't have someone on my side like that. I've *never* had that."

My heart sinks and my eyes sting. How could he say that, after everything? "You had *me*. I supported you, no matter what."

Ben's eyes soften, and he steps toward me. But if I let him touch me right now, I'll just give in to him, and that wouldn't solve anything. He has a big problem he's been hiding from me for weeks, and there's nothing I can do to fix it. This one's all on him.

I hold up my hands. "No, forget I said that. It clearly doesn't matter."

I shove past him and head for the door. He grabs my arm, but I yank it out of his grasp.

"Hannah, what are you doing?"

"Leaving."

"Seriously? Can we just talk about this?"

I shake my head. "Talk about what? You've already made up your mind without telling me. You're moving to Chicago to go to law school. That's all there is to say."

I pause at the door with my hand on the knob. I don't look at him because I won't be able to leave if I do, and I really need to leave because tears are welling up in my eyes. "Good luck, Ben. You're going to need it."

The afternoon fades into evening as I sit on my bed in my dorm room, staring at my hands in my lap. Every now and then my phone buzzes at my side, but I ignore it. I didn't exactly plan to break up with Ben, but when his first call came in, I hesitated. If I answered, he'd apologize it away, I'd pretend I didn't care, and we'd go back to being us. But he's moving away in a few short months, and he's been hiding that from me.

Maybe, all along, *I* was the one who assumed he was going to grad school here in Arlington, but he was never so sure. I'm so in love with him that I could easily take him back and ignore the truth, grateful to have him however I can. But he keeps going after what's "right" instead of what he loves. How long until that includes me? Am I just like the master's degree for him? The thing he knows he loves but can't commit to?

Ben's on some collision course with his future, and I don't want to be on board for the ride, even if it's with him. So I let his call go to voicemail. And the next one, and the next. All afternoon, it gets harder to deny him, but I do. I have to.

I miss my mom in a way I don't too often anymore. If she were here, would we talk about Ben? Would she have given me advice or comforted me as I cried? Would she have made me feel certain that I'm doing the right thing, or would she have told me I'm making a mistake?

The door slams open, light floods in, and Jasmine blows into our room. "Jesus," she gasps, slapping her hand to her chest. "You scared the shit out of me. Why are you hiding here in the dark?"

I open my mouth to respond, but I can't talk. I'm crying. I've been crying all afternoon, and my face is wet and my eyes are puffy.

"Hannah?" Jasmine rushes to my side. "What's wrong?"

"Ben," I choke out. "We…kind of had a fight."

She strokes my hair. "About what?"

"Law school."

"Is his dad still giving him grief about that?"

"He doesn't have to give him grief anymore. Ben's going."

Jasmine leans back. "Hold on. He's actually doing it? I thought he wanted to go to grad school here for lit."

"He did. He does. But he's accepted an offer to go to

law school instead, even though he knows he'll hate it. God, we've talked about it so many times, but he never said he was actually going to go."

She sighs and slips her arm around my shoulders. "Maybe he just needs to work this out for himself. You can tell him a million times it's a mistake, but until he tries it himself, he won't be convinced. This fall, when he's actually in the thick of it, he'll figure it out and—"

"He's moving to Chicago."

Jasmine grimaces.

"He applied to law school in Chicago, and he didn't say a word to me about it. So even if he finally figures it out in the fall, he won't be here."

"You know," she says gently. "People do manage to survive the long distance thing. Sean and I did it for a year. It's not the end of the world."

I shake my head. "The problem isn't Chicago. He's choosing this thing he hates because he thinks he should. How long do you think it'll take him to find a girlfriend who's a better choice than me?" As soon as the words come out, my stomach sinks, and I cover my face. "You know, Alex is going to law school, too. He always wanted her first anyway."

"Hey, you don't know it's going to go that way."

"No, but I don't want to be around to see it if it does."

I start crying again, the sobs swelling up and drowning me. Jasmine wraps her arms around me and rocks me as I cry. My phone buzzes again, and Jasmine hesitates. "Is that him?"

I nod.

"You sure you don't want to talk to him?"

"And say what? Good luck in Chicago next year? Have

fun without me? It's just…" I sit up and wipe my face. "He was the first person I talked to about the whole chem thing. And he's been there, cheering me on the whole way, even when we were just friends. But now the tables are turned, and he kept it a huge secret. Even when I asked him, he didn't tell me the truth. I don't matter enough to him to even be a part of this decision."

"Oh, Hannah… I'm so sorry."

Jasmine's pity is worse than anything. I almost wish she'd snark at me or tell me to put on more eyeliner and get over it. But who am I kidding? Right now, anything she could say would make me cry because Ben might as well already be gone.

Chapter Twenty-Five

BEN

It's snowing again. The third time this week. It's not heavy, but it's been enough to keep most of the customers away. Too bad because I could really use the distraction.

It's been a week since Hannah walked out of my apartment and not a word. I called at first—straight to voicemail. I left messages pleading with her to talk to me. Then I texted. Then I was pissed she wouldn't even hear me out and got drunk with John. And somewhere in the middle of a wretched hangover the next day, I realized she was right. About part of it at least.

I'm going to law school in Chicago in the fall, so maybe this is all for the best. Letting her go hurts more than I could possibly have imagined, but it would hurt even worse at the end of the school year, when we were in so much deeper. So maybe I should quit chasing her and let her go. She's the first of many things I have to give up.

I've felt sick since the second she walked out the door. Before that. Since my father told me in no uncertain terms that I fall in line or fall out for good.

I chase it around and around in my mind. I want Hannah, but she doesn't want this version of me. She wants the guy she fell for last fall, the idealist who handed her a book and expanded her mind. That guy gets his MA in lit, and probably his PhD, too, and spends his life talking about books. But that was a pipe dream; this is reality. Maybe the truth is, Hannah and I don't work in this reality.

The bell rings— Someone's actually here? This close to closing? I crane my neck to look around the stack of books I've been cataloging—well, trying to catalog. I want it to be Hannah in the worst way, but if she can't be bothered to answer my texts, there's not a chance she'd trudge out here in the snow just to see me.

And it's not—It's Alex, brushing snow from her shoulders as she bumps the door closed behind her. She gives me a small smile and sets a cup onto my desk.

"Hot chocolate," she says. "You think I didn't notice that you never drank the coffee? I just didn't realize you preferred hot chocolate until you ordered it with Hannah."

The mention of Hannah and hot chocolate sends me spinning back through memories, sunlight on her eyelashes, whipped cream on my lip, and her thumb in her mouth as she smiled at me. My stomach cramps as I force a smile. "Thanks, but you don't need to bribe me to come hang out here, you know. We're friends."

"I didn't come to hang out and swap retail war stories. I came to drag you out for a drink."

"A drink?" Alex and I have never hung out outside of work—unless you count the party, which I don't. This is something I always wanted before Hannah, but now? I'm not sure what to say.

She smiles. "Look, we'll both be at Chicago College in the fall. I figured we should hang out. Form our own little alliance, like on *Survivor*. I hear it's cutthroat there— It'd be nice to have a friendly face on my side."

I laugh. Finding out Alex was also accepted to Chicago College of Law was possibly the only thing about the past week that hasn't sucked. She's right, having a friend makes it marginally easier to stomach.

"Sure, a drink sounds good actually. Want to wait while I close up, or should I just meet you someplace?"

She shrugs awkwardly, which is weird for Alex, who is usually nothing but self-assured. "I'll wait for you. If that's okay."

"Yeah, whatever. It'll only take a minute."

W e end up at Smitty's because it's close and my favorite. Alex looks around as we walk in, taking in the seventies-era wood paneling, the beer lights old enough to be collector's items, and the clientele, a bunch of weathered old locals and a handful of college oddballs like me.

"Cute place," she says.

"I like it here. It's casual."

"I'll say." She follows me to a half-circle booth in the corner. It's too early for the evening crowd, so it's pretty empty. Alex eyes the cracked vinyl seat for a second before sliding in next to me. We order a pitcher of beer, which is cold, cheap, and delicious, and spend a few minutes talking about the admissions process. Well, Alex talks, and I listen. She agonized and sweated over her application and took the LSATs three times to maximize her scores. I wrote a half-assed personal statement in less time than it takes to order a pizza, and a friend of my dad's did the rest. It's actually really shitty that I got in at all when there were applicants like her working their asses off.

"So," she says. "I haven't seen Hannah around lately."

I wince—hearing her name still hurts. Kind of feels like it always will. "Um, we... I guess we broke up."

"You guess?"

"We did." Not because I wanted to. Not because I don't want her.

"Okay," Alex says, and then she draws in a deep breath. "So maybe we should go out sometime. Or now. We could be out now. Like a date."

I stare at her, blinking stupidly. Did Alex just ask me out? *Me?* Shit, are we on a date now? How the hell did this happen?

"Um... What about Chip?"

"Oh, him." She shrugs dismissively. "Turns out we were in an open relationship, and I was the only one who didn't know it." She laughs. "See? I told you I have terrible taste in men. But I was thinking about all these assholes I go out with and telling myself I need to find a nice guy to date, and I realized I already know a perfectly nice guy. I figured maybe I should try dating him."

"Well, that's really...um..." To be honest, the way she put it is slightly off-putting, like I'm a default "nice guy" to try out for some social experiment. But I think I get where she's coming from, even if the way she asked was clumsy.

Alex charges on, filling the gap as I fumble for something to say. "And since we'll both be at Chicago College in the fall, it just makes sense."

"It does?"

"Sure. We already know each other. We already get along great. We're going to the same law school in the fall, and we have the same goals."

I'm half expecting her to pull out her laptop and give me a PowerPoint presentation about all the ways her and me together is a great idea, but that last thing she said is hanging me up. I'm pretty sure Alex and I don't have the same goals at all. Not really.

I must be an idiot, because the girl I wanted for nearly a year is sitting here with me, saying she also wants me. And she's right; we'd make sense together. But I don't want any of it. Not law school and not Alex— Everything in me still belongs to Hannah.

"So what do you say? I think we could be good for each other, have some laughs—"

"Alex, I'm sorry." I can't believe that after a year of pining for her, I'm the one letting her down easy.

"Oh. You're not broken up with Hannah?"

"No, we are. It's just…"

She sits back and smiles ruefully. "Ah. You're still in love with her."

My heart stutters. Still in love with Hannah? "I am?"

"Aren't you?"

My head falls forward, and I squeeze my eyes shut. Of course I am. Feelings like these don't just disappear when the other person leaves you. That'd be too easy. "I guess I am."

Alex hesitates, then leans forward onto her elbows. "What happened? If you don't mind my asking."

"I kept a big secret from her."

"You could apologize. Hannah's seriously nice, and frankly, she adores you. I'm sure if you talked to her, she'd reconsider."

Considering Alex has gone from asking me out to giving me advice on winning back my ex in the space of five minutes, I'm guessing she wasn't all that romantically invested in me in the first place. Which actually makes me feel better— Maybe she's realized we're better off as friends.

But of course, that doesn't really solve the problem. "It wouldn't matter. I still have to do what I was hiding, and when I do, I'll lose her anyway."

"Which is?"

"Law school. I didn't tell her I was applying. In fact, I told her I wasn't going. And when she found out, she was rightfully furious."

Alex scowls. "Well, if it's what you want to do with your life, she could try being supportive."

I can't help it. I laugh— It's just so ridiculous looking at it ass-backward. "But it's not. That's what she's really mad about."

Alex looks even more confused. "Wait… You don't want to go?"

"No. It was my dad's plan. He'll cut me off if I don't go and…" I sigh and shake my head. "He's probably right. Law school is the smart thing to do."

She narrows those sharp, ice-blue eyes at me. Damn,

Alex'll make a kick-ass trial lawyer because she hasn't said a word, and I'm already sweating like a defendant on the stand. "You're seriously going to go to one of the toughest law schools in the country to make somebody *else* happy? Ben, that's insane."

"Yeah, but my dad has a point. A master's in English Lit isn't going to make me rich. At least law is like, a thing."

A smile slowly overtakes Alex's face. She chuckles and shakes her head.

"What?"

"An MA in lit is so *you*. Now that you put it in my head, it's all I can see. Oh, you could be a professor! That would be *perfect* for you. I can't even imagine you at law school now."

I frown. "Thanks a lot."

"No, not like that." She touches my arm, but there's nothing to it. No spark, no heat. Not like when Hannah touches me. "You're smart. You could totally do it. It would just be so *wrong*."

I hesitate. Hannah said almost the same thing, months ago. She even said I'd make a great teacher. "But I'd be cut off. How could I ever pay for it?"

Alex shrugs and sips her beer. "If it's what you want to do with your life, shouldn't you try to find a way? And it means getting the girl you're in love with back. Sounds worth the effort to me. I mean, I'd have moved mountains to get into Chicago College. Do you want it that bad?"

Doing what I love for the rest of my life and winning back Hannah? Of course I want it that bad. But can I have it? Do I have what it takes to make it happen?

It all comes down to this, doesn't it? What I want versus what others want from me. What I choose now will determine how I live the rest of my life. It seems so simple, so painfully obvious, that I don't know why I ever thought I could make another choice.

Of course, it won't be that simple. Or easy. But Alex is right. I have to give it everything I've got, no matter how hard it is. My life is worth it. Hannah is worth it.

Chapter Twenty-Six

HANNAH

The World of Books near campus couldn't be more different than Prometheus; it's hard to believe the two stores serve the same function. I wander the aisles, looking for something to read. I haven't picked up a book since I walked out of Ben's apartment a week ago, and it's driving me crazy. I'm desperate to get lost in someone else's world for a while, so I've waded into the superstore, even though buying a book without Ben physically hurts.

The store is massive, with soaring high ceilings and bright fluorescent lighting. The shelves are glossy, pale wood lined with tidy, dust-free stacks of books with multiple copies of each title. Printed tags identify some as best sellers or award-winners. Every book is clean and new, without battered dust jackets, dog-eared pages, or notes scribbled inside front covers or along the margins. They're all blank slates, created to be read fresh, without history to share.

Round tables are scattered everywhere with books grouped by theme. Non-fiction, crime, young adult fantasy, book club favorites, and beach reads even though it's winter in Ohio and the beach is a distant memory. They make it so easy to find exactly what you want to read, so why am I still wandering the store in a fog?

Nothing grabs my attention. I don't want to know how many weeks this book topped the New York Times Bestseller list, or when the blockbuster film adaptation is being released. I want to know what Ben thought about it. I want Ben to describe it to me, his eyes alight with excitement. I want a book that Ben has picked out especially for me, because he knows me and knows it'll be exactly the one I want and need to read right now. But Ben isn't here, instead an army of World of Books employees in identical red polo shirts are. And not one of them looks like they would happily spend an hour picking out the perfect book for me to read.

Without Ben, there isn't any excitement to this process. I'm not searching this room full of books, mind spinning with possibilities like in Prometheus. Even with the burned out bulbs, the dust, the rickety, mismatched, overstuffed shelves, Prometheus felt magical. Here I could just as easily be buying canned soup or T-shirts.

I miss him so much, and I could have him back with a phone call. I'm not even all that mad that he kept law school a secret from me anymore. He was under a freakish amount of pressure from his dickhead dad, and he knew what I'd say, so he didn't want to tell me. I get it. But he's still moving to Chicago in a few months and starting a new life that's the antithesis of everything he cares about. It's going to change him, and I can't bear to watch him become someone new. I love the old Ben too much.

I don't buy anything. There's nothing here I want. It's snowing again outside, coating the dirty heaps already on the ground with a fresh, clean layer of white. I walk without a destination as I watch my feet sink into the snow, one step after the other, over the Tenumbrah River and into downtown Arlington. The sparkling twinkle lights strung up for the holidays have all been packed away. The magic is gone.

I've actively avoided going anywhere near Prometheus since I walked out on Ben. But it's like my feet are hardwired to go there, and I'm turning onto Charles Street before registering where I've been headed. Now that I'm here, I just want to walk by and catch a glimpse of him, to see if he looks as bad as I feel.

Halfway up the block, he steps out the door, and a second later, Alex exits behind him. She's chattering away about something, laughing, while Ben smiles and nods and goes through the routine of closing up the shop.

Well, I wanted to torture myself, and now I'm getting what I wanted, because this is *awful*. I can't breathe. I can't move a muscle. More than anything, I want to run away, but I can't stop looking.

Ben finishes closing the store, and they chat for a minute. Ben shrugs offhandedly and motions up the street in the opposite direction from me. Alex smiles at him. He's not looking at her, so he doesn't see it, but I do. She's fucking flirting with him.

After another moment, they turn and walk away side by side.

I told Jasmine it was a possibility that he and Alex might be together in law school next year, since she'd mentioned applying to the same school he's going to. I thought maybe he'd remember how much he wanted her before he met me. Seems I was right.

I stand there long after they've disappeared from sight. The truth is obvious: Ben has already started down that new path he chose. And he might have started me down my own path, but it's clear I need to follow it alone.

Chapter Twenty-Seven

BEN

Candlelight glints off the hefty silver cutlery and wine-glasses filled with a very expensive Cabernet. Heavy, white plates laden with perfectly prepared steaks rest on a thick, snowy tablecloth in one of the best steakhouses in Chicago.

My father set up this "celebratory" dinner to thank Richard as soon as the call came in about my acceptance. I didn't cancel it, even after my enlightening conversation with Alex.

I've fucked up—in many ways and for a long time. But the biggest mistake I've made is living in fear. I have a long list of things I need to do, but this one is a top priority. If I'm going to go for it, I can't have the security of law school and a trust fund to fall back on. I don't want the temptation of taking the path of least resistance when things get hard. If

I'm finally going to be brave enough to claim my own future;
I'm doing it without a safety net.

"Once you get to the spring semester, we can start looking for an internship with a firm or a clerkship with a judge
for next summer," Richard says.

My father leans forward and stabs his fork into a blood-
red slice of steak. "You want an internship with a good firm,
Ben." He points his dripping steak at me. "None of this
clerkship stuff. Knowing you, you'll end up working as a
damn public defender if you go that route."

"Public defenders play a vital role in the system," Richard says evenly.

It sucks that I have to drag him into our drama—he's
actually a friendly, decent guy, despite being old friends with
my dad—but the only way Dad will get it is if I make it irre-
vocable, and for that, I need witnesses. This isn't some minor
Ben rebellion he can crush and sweep under the family rug.
This is a full-out revolution. Go big or go home, right? Well,
after tonight, I won't have a home, so I'm going *really* big.
All this time I've been looking for a way around his ulti-
matum, but the answer is clear. I don't need to go around—
I need to bust straight through it and stop worrying about
what'll break when I do.

"Sure, public defenders are useful," my father agrees.
"For folks who need them. And that's fine for all those lib-
eral arts types, but Ben here has a hell of a brain. He'll do
great in civil law. Right, Ben?"

I inhale deeply. Now's the time. The opening is right here
in front of me. If I back out now, I'll never have the courage
to do what I need to do. So I straighten my shoulders, look
Dad straight in the eye, and say, "No."

"Excuse me?" he says, a note of warning in his voice.

I put my fork down. "I won't do great in civil law or criminal law or any other kind. I mean, yeah, I could muddle through if I wanted to, but I'm not going to because I'm not going to be a lawyer."

"Now Ben," my dad says smoothly. "We've talked about this."

"No, *you've* talked, and I've gone along with it because I was scared, but I'm done with that. This isn't right. I don't want to be a lawyer. I know what I want to do with my life, and this isn't it."

"I thought we put the teaching nonsense to bed," Dad snaps.

"You did. I haven't. I won't."

Richard shifts uncomfortably. "If you'd like me to give you a moment—"

"That's not necessary, Richard. Ben's just—"

I stand, throwing my white linen napkin onto my untouched plate. "Ben's finally fucking speaking up for himself."

My dad's voice drops into an ominous register. "You know what happens if you fuck this up, sport." Unease flickers through me, but I shove it away. That's an old reaction, left over from childhood. I'm about to lay claim to my adulthood. It's long overdue.

"Yeah, I know, you'll cut me off, disown me, whatever. Do what you want, but I'm not going to law school."

Dad glares at me, his face turning an ugly shade of purple. "Exactly what do you think you're going to do if you walk out of here?"

"I'll catch a bus back to Arlington. I have a lot of stuff to fix, but it's about time I started living my life for me, don't you think?" I turn to Richard and extend my hand. "Richard, I'm sorry. You were really great. Thank you for everything, but I can't do this."

Richard hesitates, then smiles and shakes my hand. "Don't worry about it, Ben. Good luck with everything."

My dad snorts in disgust. "He's going to need luck. I swear, Ben, you won't see a dime from me."

"I know, Dad. If I walk out, it'll be big and bad and permanent. But for better or for worse, it'll be mine. I'll roll the dice, and I'll play whatever comes up. You're an investor—You should appreciate that, right?"

I don't wait to hear his reaction. I turn and walk out of the restaurant into the freezing Chicago night. For the first time in ages, I can breathe.

Chapter Twenty-Eight

HANNAH

"Jasmine, are these yours? They were in my laundry when I brought it back upstairs." I hold up a tiny pair of lacy, red panties.

Her eyes light up. "That's where they went! Sean's going to be so excited. They're his favorite."

"Spare me the details, please."

Jasmine's touching up her makeup at lightning speed, getting ready to head out to a party hosted by Sean's team. I'm doing my laundry on a Friday night. Of course.

"Hey, can I ask you something, Jasmine?"

"Sure, shoot."

"So I talked to the guidance counselor today, and they approved my request to do a late drop."

Jasmine turns away from her mirror to look at me. "What are you dropping?"

I take a deep breath, keeping my eyes on my neatly folded T-shirts. "The two classes from the Chemistry curriculum I was taking."

"So you're really pulling the plug?"

I look up in alarm. "You don't think I'm making a mistake, do you?"

She laughs. "No, you moved on from chemistry way back last fall when you cracked open that first novel. Glad to see you owning it now. What are you adding in its place?"

"I talked to the professor of Selected Works of British Lit today, and she agreed to let me in if I get a tutor to help me catch up."

A slow smile spreads across Jasmine's face. "I knew it. Hannah Gregory, English major."

I shake my head. "I'm not sure yet. I just want to take some of the classes this year and I'll see. I might still change my mind."

"I don't think so," she singsongs. "Hannah's finally found her passion. It's too bad—"

Her face falls as she bites off the word, but I know what she was about to say. *It's too bad Ben isn't here,* because I'd have never found my way here without him. And he won't even know.

"Sorry, Hannah, I didn't mean—"

I swallow hard and look away. "It's okay."

She hesitates. "Have you heard from him?"

I shake my head and fight back tears. I've been so good lately, and I'm not going to break down now.

"I didn't expect to. And now I really won't."

"What do you mean?"

I peek at her. "I saw him coming out of Prometheus."

She glares at me. "I thought we agreed you weren't going to go there anymore."

"I know, and I wasn't. I just ended up on that street, and he was closing the store. Alex was with him."

"Oh. Are they…?"

I shrug, hoping I look far less devastated than I feel. "I don't know. But it looks like they'll be together in law school next year, so it makes sense. She's perfect for him."

"So were you," she says gently.

I shake my head. "For some version of himself he's leaving behind, maybe."

Jasmine sits down and puts an arm around me. "I know it sucks, but just focus on yourself right now, Hannah. So many great things are happening for you."

As hard as it is, she's right. I can't keep dwelling on what I lost. Not when there's so much still out there waiting for me to explore.

Chapter Twenty-Nine

Ben

The English Department is the first stop I make when I get back to Arlington. I want to go straight to Hannah, but I'm still empty-handed. As long as I've known her, she's seen the very best version of me, even when I didn't believe that guy existed. I'm doing everything I can to bring him back to life, but I don't want to just *tell* her I'm different, I need to *show* her. And for that, there are a few things I need to do first.

I catch Professor Donnelly right between classes. It's a madhouse, with students pushing their way out of class as others try to push their way in. I squeeze behind a guy and reach Donnelly as he puts his notes back into his briefcase.

"Hey, Professor Donnelly, can I talk to you for a minute?"

The professor looks up and smiles at me. "Only a minute,

I'm afraid. Class starts soon."

"Right. Sorry. It's about grad school next year."

He nods. "You submitted your application, didn't you?"

"I did." That was my first act of rebellion, sending that application in on Thanksgiving Day. Here I am, finally seeing it through.

"Then there's nothing to worry about. Your acceptance should be a fairly straightforward business. I believe the letters are going out in the next couple weeks. "

"It's not getting in that's the problem. It's the money." I pause and swallow thickly. "My financial situation has changed, and I'm going to have less support than I expected."

"I see." Donnelly rubs a finger across his chin. "And by 'less,' you mean…"

"None. I'm doing it on my own."

"Oh dear. It's quite a lot of money, you understand."

I sigh. "I know. I really want to do this. I'm just not sure how to manage it."

"Well, it's not hopeless. There may be something we can do. There are a number of graduate assistantships available. Tuition would be reduced, or in some cases waived entirely in exchange for undergraduate teaching duties."

"Teaching?"

Donnelly smirks. "The Intro to Composition classes normally. You'd be showing freshmen how to properly employ a semi-colon. I'm afraid it's terribly unglamorous."

"I wouldn't mind that. Do you think I'd qualify for a graduate assistantship?"

"I'm happy to make the recommendation. The aid office awards them based on need however."

I chuckle. "Well, I'm in need, that's for sure. I'm on my

own and pretty much penniless."

"Then odds are good that you'll get one to cover at least part of your tuition. Of course, it won't help with living expenses. You'd have to cover that with some sort of outside funds."

My mind spins, calculating just how cheaply I can live for the next several years. I've taken my father's money for granted all my life. Now I'm out on a tightrope without a net, with only my own wits and hard work to depend on.

"I'll see what I can do."

"I'll email you some information about the assistantship application. You should have a talk with the financial aid department as soon as possible so you can begin establishing your need."

I smile. "Thank you, Professor. I really appreciate your help."

"I wish there was more I could do. You've got a lot of promise, Ben. I hope you can work this out and be a part of the program."

"Me, too. I'd better go. I've got some other plans to make."

"Good luck, Ben."

The words steal my breath for a second. That's the last thing Hannah said to me before she walked out. She said I'd need it, and I do. Luck and a whole lot of hard work, apparently. Donnelly's next class is starting, so I clear out. I have a few more things to get lined up before I can fix the most important thing I broke.

Chapter Thirty

As I stare at the hundreds of pages of reading I have to get through, my eyeballs want to turn inside out. But I talked my way into this English Lit class several weeks after the semester started, so it's on me to catch up. I love it, I do, but I wish I didn't have to love quite so much of it all at once.

Jasmine is lying on her bed on her stomach, reading her Intro to World Cultures book and pointedly not indulging my need for a distraction. This is why Jasmine will rule the world one day; she physically *can't* procrastinate.

There's a knock on our door, and I start to get up, but Jasmine stops me with a look.

"No way. I'll get it. You finish reading."

She's really no fun at all, but I refocus on *Beowulf* with a sigh. Jasmine rounds the corner into the vestibule where the door is.

"Hey, you must be Jasmine," the visitor says. That voice is familiar, but I can't quite place it.

"Can I help you with something?" Jasmine asks. Her voice is sharp, and I can almost see the withering stare she's giving the guy.

"I'm just dropping something off for Hannah."

I scramble off the bed and hurry to the vestibule. She's blocking the door like a one-woman army, but it's John, Ben's roommate. My heart plunges. Why the hell has *John* come to see me?

"John, what are you… Is Ben okay?"

He cracks a small smile. "Ben's fine. He just asked me to bring you this."

John holds out a present with almost more tape than wrinkled wrapping paper. Jasmine looks like she'd like to lop off John's arm as he reaches past her to hand it to me. Judging from the shape and weight, it's a book. Ben picked out another book for me?

"Why…" I take a shaky breath. "Why didn't he bring it himself?"

John smiles again and shakes his head. "I don't know a thing. Just open your book, Hannah. I'll see you around, okay? See you, Jasmine."

She snorts dismissively and closes the door in his face, then rounds on me. "What is it?"

I carry the package back to my bed. My hands are shaking, and I really need to sit down. "A book."

Her eyes narrow. "Why is he giving you a book?"

"He always gave me books," I whisper.

She drops down onto my bed next to me. "Well, open it!"

Easier said than done. I have to break through all the tape first, but finally I wrestle it free and flip it over to read the cover. *Infinite Jest* by David Foster Wallace. A used copy. A *very* used copy. It's got dozens of dog-eared corners and little slips of paper are tucked everywhere between the pages. I thumb the edges and gloss over hundreds of penciled notes in the margins in Ben's handwriting. This is *his* book, not just a copy from the store.

I open the front cover, and a piece of paper flutters into my lap.

Dear Hannah,

Do you remember the first time you came into Prometheus? I'll never forget that day. You asked me which book was my favorite, and I laughed and said that was an impossible question. But that was an academic answer, and the truth is, I do have a favorite book, one I love more than anything I've ever read. This is the one. I've read it a thousand times, but now, more than ever, I'd like to read it with you. Reading everything is better with you.

If you think you can forgive me, you know where to find me. Until then, I'll be waiting for you.

Love,

Ben

My eyes burn, and my throat aches with the tears I'm determined not to shed. The words blur on the page as I blink, trying to hold it in. I stare at his note, rereading it while Jasmine unabashedly peers over my shoulder.

"He wants to read it with you?" she says. "What the hell does that mean?"

I throw my hands in the air. "I have no idea! What am I supposed to do with that? What does he want?"

Jasmine takes the copy of *Infinite Jest* and flips dismissively through the pages. "If he was going to send you a book, the least he could do was buy you a new copy."

Despite my confusion and rioting emotions, I rescue it from her and then cradle it in my lap. "No, it's better used."

"It is?"

"It has more than one story to tell."

She just stares at me. I flip through the book again, skimming all the things Ben has said about this book during his rereads, all his thoughts tucked into the pages alongside the words.

"What's the other story it's telling?" Jasmine finally asks.

"I'm not sure," I whisper. "But I think I need to find out." I stuff the book into my messenger bag and reach for my coat.

"Wait a minute," Jasmine protests. "Where are you going?"

I point at my bag because it's so obvious, at least to me. "Prometheus."

She frowns. "Are you sure that's a good idea? He's already hurt you plenty."

I nod. "And it might hurt some more. But I won't know unless I go. He's trying to say something. I should at least find out what it is."

She still looks skeptical. "Do you want me to come along? I'm excellent at ass-kicking."

I smile. "I appreciate the offer, but I'm pretty sure this is just between Ben and me."

"Don't…"

I raise an eyebrow at her, waiting for the rest.

She sighs. "Just be careful. You're finally starting to figure out what you want. Don't forget all of that just for him."

"I won't."

"And call me. I want details."

When I left our dorm room, I was sure I needed to do this, but as I get closer to Prometheus, my confidence flags. I'm not sure what Ben is trying to say with that note. He misses me? Misses reading with me? Yeah, me, too. But what is he asking? Does he want to try to recapture that despite what's happened and what he's chosen? I can't do that. And if he suggests we go back to being *friends*, there's no way on earth I'm agreeing.

I don't know what he means, and I won't until I ask him, which means I need to go in the store. The unassuming wood and glass door of Prometheus hovers in front of me like a gauntlet to be run.

I'll be okay. Seeing him, talking to him, might be hard. Hell, it might be awful. But if there's one thing I learned from this year of not talking to my dad about what mattered, it's that keeping it all inside doesn't solve anything, and in the end, it eats you away. For better or for worse, I need to face Ben.

I take a deep breath, seize the door handle, yank the door open, and stride into the store, the tiny bell tinkling as I enter.

Ben seems to be the only person inside, and he's behind the register, typing something into the computer. My stupid heart flops hopelessly in my chest. God, I miss him.

He looks up at the bell, and his face transforms. His dark eyes widen, and if my heart plunged when I saw him, it stops completely when I lock eyes with him. Everything about him is so precious and familiar. His dark hair is too long and a mess, his glasses are slightly askew, and he probably hasn't shaved today. He looks perfect.

"Hannah," he says on an exhale, like he can scarcely believe I'm here. He scrambles out from behind the counter, hurries across the front of the store, and stops just a couple feet away. "You came."

I pull his book from my bag. "I got your present."

"Did you like it?"

I scowl. "I'm not sure I understand it. Why did you give me this? And why did you make John bring it?"

He looks down at the floor, fidgeting nervously. "I wanted to talk to you here. It felt right. This place is… It's us, you know?"

My eyes burn but I won't cry. How dare he say stuff like that to me now? I swallow hard to keep the tears at bay. "Yeah, it was."

Ben winces at the past tense. "Look, Hannah." He takes a deep breath, like he's about to jump into deep, cold water. "I'm sorry. I was totally and completely wrong. I was an idiot."

I frown. "About which part?"

"For the law school thing. For not telling you about the law school thing. I kept thinking I'd figure out a way out of it and wouldn't have to tell you, but there wasn't a way out. And I should have told you. You deserved my honesty."

I hesitate. "You're right. It was shitty not to tell me about it. You treated me like a kid you couldn't trust."

He shakes his head sadly. "I never thought of you as a kid, not even when I tried to."

"I've been handling some adult shit for a long time. I could have handled your stuff, too, if you'd just told me about it." My raw emotions bubble to the surface, and my eyes sting again.

Ben winces and looks at his feet. "I know. I'm sorry. I think the last few months have proved that you're much better at handling life stuff than I am."

Seeing the slump of his shoulders and the strain and defeat in his voice snuffs out that last tiny flare of anger. He's really sorry—staying mad at him would just be spiteful and won't change anything. I sigh. "It's okay."

Ben looks up again, examining me closely. "Okay?"

I look down at the copy of *Infinite Jest*. I think I get it now. It was his peace offering, showing me he values what we had in the beginning, even if it didn't work out. I value it, too—more than he'll ever realize. "I appreciate the apology. I hope it works out for you."

He frowns. "You hope what works out?"

"Law school. Good luck. I really mean that this time."

"Oh." Ben shifts and smiles slightly, reaching up to scratch behind his ear. "About that… I'm not going."

I blink. What the hell is he talking about? All of this happened because he *had* to go. And just like that, now he's not? "What do you mean? Did you not get in or something?"

"No, I got in. But I'm not going."

He sounds really sure of himself—resolved, even. When we broke up, he told me he didn't have a choice. So what changed?

"What about your dad?"

"He's fucking furious. I don't think he's speaking to me anymore. I haven't exactly called to check."

"But what about the money? I thought you said he'd cut you off."

"He did. I mean, I assume so. Like I said, we haven't talked to nail down the details of my banishment."

I can't believe what he's saying. Ben just cut all ties with his family to avoid going to law school? But I suppose he's always known exactly who he is—He knew in his heart law school was a mistake. With this huge step, everything's different now.

"What are you going to do?"

"Graduate school, here at Arlington State. Like I wanted." His eyes are bright with excitement, but I don't miss the nervous smile.

"How?"

"I've applied for a graduate assistantship, which will hopefully help a lot. And I'll have to work my ass off to pay for the rest."

"You already put in a million hours here, Ben. You couldn't work more here if you tried."

"Well, that's the other thing. I just put in my notice."

"Your notice for what?"

"I quit Prometheus. I was writing up a handbook for whoever replaces me when you came in. Ralph's hiring, if you're interested."

I open my mouth to say something, but no words come out. This store without Ben just doesn't exist in my mind. Why would he do something so drastic, something that must have been painful for him? "But you *love* it here."

He looks around wistfully. "I do, but Ralph pays for shit. He's the first to admit it. I need to make more now that I'm actually supporting myself. It's fine. He gets it."

"What are you gonna do instead?"

He grins at me—a smile that still gives me butterflies—and reaches into his pocket. He pulls out a laminated red nametag from World of Books with his name on it.

I gasp. "No way!" I snatch it out of his hand to examine it. It's the real thing, brand new and shiny and reads, "Ben, World of Books Sales Associate."

"I thought you hated this place!"

"I *did* hate them. Now I'm a member of the World of Books team. They might be soulless, capitalist swine, but they pay pretty well. Plus they have benefits. I'm pretty sure I just got kicked off my parents' health insurance."

I laugh in disbelief. "Jesus, you're serious about this."

"Yeah, I am."

I hand his tag back and beam at him. "Wow, that's great. You're really going after this." I'm so proud of him for coming to his senses and fighting for his dream.

"That's not all I'm going after." Ben takes a deep breath and points to the book he sent me. "I didn't send that to you just because I thought you'd find it entertaining, Hannah."

I look down at the ratty book in my hands.

"That book is probably my most prized possession," he says. "And I want you to have it."

I don't know what to say, but I don't need to, because Ben's not done. "Hannah, I'm sorry about everything. But the thing I'm most sorry about is losing you."

"Ben, I—"

"Just let me say this. You were right to walk out on me. I was fucking up hopelessly. A year from now, or maybe two years or five or ten, I'd have looked around and not recognized myself. It took losing you to make me see what I was doing, what I was losing, and for something that was so...*screw* the money. That's not important, but you're everything. I quit all of it—the money, law school, my shitty family, Prometheus—just hoping I could get back the one thing that really mattered. You."

I shake my head. While this whole thing makes my heart want to explode, it's too much. "Ben, you can't do all that just for me."

He smiles. "I know. I did it for me, so I can be the guy you fell for last fall and not the asshole who screwed it up last month. I don't want to live the rest of my life as that guy. You always saw the very best version of me, Hannah. I'll do whatever it takes to be him. For you, but also for me."

I can't fight back tears anymore. They slip from under my lashes, streaking down my face. He's saying every right and perfect thing, but he was about to turn his back on me once to do what he thought was right, and I'm still scared he might do it again. After all there was—

"What about Alex?"

Ben frowns. "Alex? What does she have to do with anything?"

"I saw you with her," I blurt out.

Ben looks confused for a second, and then he bursts out laughing. "Oh, no. I mean, yeah, there was an awkward minute or two, but I didn't—and she didn't really—and just... no. Actually, Alex was the one to shake some fucking sense into me."

"What?"

"She pointed out, very wisely, that I'm still in love with you, and I'd be an idiot to let you get away just to follow somebody else's dream."

"Oh." It comes out as more of a breathy sigh than a word. "That was very smart of her."

"Alex is smart. But not for me." Ben reaches out and brushes a tear off my cheek, and his hand lingers, almost cupping my face but not quite. All the nerve endings in my skin come alive at the gentle touch of his fingers. "I've already found the girl for me. I just hope I haven't fucked it up too badly to fix."

He says it like a question, and I want to tell him no, it's not too late, but I can't speak because I'm crying too hard. Ben hesitantly reaches for me with his other hand and holds my face gently in his palms.

"It's not going to be easy, Hannah. I'm going to have to work every waking hour next year just to keep my head above water. I don't have a single thing to offer but that stupid used book. But I hope you'll take it, and me. Because if you'll start over with me, I'll try my damndest to deserve it this time."

My fingers worry the ragged edges of *Infinite Jest*. "Will this book change my life?" I whisper.

Ben tries to suppress his smile and fails miserably. "I hope it changes your *whole* life."

Then Ben pulls me into his arms and kisses me, crushing the book between us. And oh, I've missed this. The way he turns my knees to jelly every time our lips touch, the feel of our breath mingling together, and wow, I've really missed that thing he does with his tongue. He slides one hand back to cradle my head, his fingers tangling in my hair, and kisses me harder. All the pent up wanting, all that desperation from being apart comes through in that kiss.

I want to drag him out of here, back to his apartment

where we can make up properly, or maybe even just upstairs to the loft, but the stupid little brass bell over the door tinkles, announcing the arrival of a customer.

We pull back, both of us dazed and a little flushed, staring at each other. The customer clears their throat, and I tear my eyes away from Ben's gorgeous face and ruffled hair to see who's come in.

A man stands just inside the door, and I'm pretty sure wherever he was headed, wandering into Prometheus was a mistake, because he doesn't belong here at all. He's tall, well over six feet, and broad, in a brawny, thick-necked way. His sandy blond hair is cropped and conservative, matching his expensive-looking gray suit and black wool overcoat. His shiny leather shoes stand out harshly against Prometheus's faded, scuffed oak floors. What could Prometheus have to offer this guy?

Ben coughs softly. I wait for him to give his polite "Can I help you, sir?" But instead, he says, "Dad? What are you doing here?"

Chapter Thirty-One

BEN

D ad looks utterly out of place surrounded by heaps of dusty, old books that feel like home to me. He's never been in Prometheus before— Hell, he hasn't been to Arlington at all outside of dropping me off freshman year and the first parents' weekend.

I haven't spoken to him since I walked out of that restaurant in Chicago. I've done my best to focus on what I needed to do and not to dwell on my family drama. But the drama must be ongoing if my father is standing in the middle of fucking Prometheus.

Dad's eyes flick from me to Hannah and back again, and he shakes his head.

"Should have known this was all about some goddamn girl."

"What? Dad, is everything okay?"

He narrows his eyes and cocks his head slightly. "You're going to ask me that after the way you walked out on dinner with Richard?"

I so don't want to do this now. My whole body is still vibrating from this thing with Hannah. I can still taste her on my lips, and I'm fucking giddy that she's back and standing beside me. All I want to do is focus on her and fix us, but instead I have to deal with my father right in front of her. Dread settles in my gut. There's no way this will go well.

I take a deep breath. "I didn't see much point in staying, since you had no intention of listening to a damn word I said."

He glares. "You threw your whole life away, caused a scene, and embarrassed the hell out of me, and you're going to stand there and say that to me?"

I clench my fists. He's come in here determined to start a fight, so if that's what he wants, so be it. "All I did was tell you about my plans for school. You're the one who wouldn't accept it and said I was wasting my life because I want to teach."

"Because you are!" His voice is so loud it practically rattles the windows. Thank God there are no customers in the store right now—until the bell tinkles softly and Alex comes in. She soundlessly slips behind my father and hovers near the front of the store, gaze flitting from my father to me.

"Dad, just calm down. Let's go talk—"

"With all the opportunities we've given you, you still want to waste your time—"

"Ben is *not* wasting his time." Hannah's quiet, steady voice cuts straight through his bluster.

I can't believe my dad can even hear her over his own

noise, but he stops mid-tirade and looks her up and down dismissively.

"This is the girl, huh? I thought if you were throwing your life away for some chick, she'd be more—"

"Stop right there. Seriously, don't say another word about her."

His eyes narrow again as he examines her, and I want to fucking lay him out for looking at her like that. "This one's a little young for you, isn't she?"

The rage wells up in me hot and overwhelming. I'm used to his judgment about me, but when he looks at Hannah that way? No fucking way.

"I'm nearly nineteen—" Hannah starts to protest, but I cut her off.

"Get the fuck out of here," I tell my dad.

"Excuse me?"

"I said get out of this store. It's one thing to yell at me— we're family and I have to put up with your bullshit—but don't you dare talk about Hannah like that."

But Dad is undeterred. "I came down here to talk some sense into you, and I'm not leaving until I do."

I'm exhausted. It's almost laughable how fucking pig-headed he is. He's so sure he can buy me because he buys anything he wants. This isn't even about what's best for me anymore; he just can't stand to lose.

"Dad." I rub my eyes under my glasses. "It's pointless. You won't convince me, and you can't bully me. I know you don't get this"—I sweep a hand around the store—"but this is who I am. It's who I've always been, who I always will be. The person you imagined me to be never existed. I'm not asking for your damn money— I'm going to pay my own way through grad school. I'd like your support, but if you're not going to give it, then you need to leave."

He lets out a disbelieving scoff. "This." He gestures at the store, the books that have been my whole life, and even Hannah, who's become the center of my life. "This is what you want to waste yourself on."

"Mr. Fisher," Hannah says tensely. "With all due respect, you're an idiot."

His eyes narrow as he looks at Hannah. "Excuse me?"

"Your son is one of the most amazing people I've ever met, and you act like he's some epic disappointment." She steps forward, facing off with him even though he dwarfs her. But the height difference doesn't matter because she's crackling with energy—even *I'm* a little intimidated by her.

"Ben knows nearly every book in this store. *Every one*. He's so passionate about them that it spills over to other people. And you don't even know what he's done for me. I was lost, and Ben gave me the perfect book, and it changed my life— *He* changed my life. He's going to be an amazing teacher. People will remember him, and not because he won some stupid case in court. He's got way more to offer the world, and it's sad you can't see how special he is."

I stare at Hannah in the silence that follows. We were still in the middle of making up or whatever it was we were doing when my dad walked in. It seemed like we were headed in the right direction, and there was that *kiss*... But if I had lingering doubts about our future, Hannah just blew them to bits. She defended me to my father like someone who loves me. I didn't think I could love her more, but I was wrong.

I grin as I take her hand. God, I love her and want to

spend every day proving it to her.

"And he's nice," Alex says, standing near the counter. "He's the nicest guy I know, even to people who don't deserve it." She winks at me, then turns sternly back to my father. "It might not mean much to you, Mr. Fisher, but you raised a nice guy, and there aren't nearly enough of them in the world. The world already has too many lawyers, and he'd make a lousy one anyway. But he'll be a kick-ass English professor and a stand-up guy. And just so we're clear, that's pretty great."

Dad eyes Alex, but she's already turned away from him. She made her case.

"Loyal, too." Adele chimes in. Where did she come from? She's materialized from the back of the store to stand behind Hannah. She tips her head back to peer up at my father from underneath her reading glasses. Dad is all red-faced, bristling outrage, but it's Adele who commands the hushed room with her quiet strength.

"Very few would give their heart and soul to a store like this one the way Ben has for four years. For what he was paid here, no one would have faulted him if he just showed up and did his time. But Ben puts his heart into everything he does. He put in his notice, and he's still making sure everything's going to go okay when he's gone. The world would be a better place with more men like your son. And all you can see is what you think is wrong with him. What a shame."

Dad's jaw works as he grinds his teeth together. No one says anything as his eyes flick between us. I can't believe Hannah, Alex, and Adele all leaped to my defense. I've never felt so accepted and grateful.

Finally, my dad plants a hand onto his hip and sighs. He

drags the other hand through his hair, and when he looks up at me, he seems smaller. Like maybe for the first time in his life, his place in the world isn't as clear to him.

"I'm not paying for it," he says, resigned. "You do this and it's on you."

"I'm not asking you to pay for it. I'm applying for a graduate assistantship, and I've got a job to pay for the rest. I'm doing this on my own."

He gives one small, tight nod, then glances at Hannah, Adele, and Alex. "I still don't understand this. I probably never will."

I shrug. "That's fair. I don't understand what you do, either. You don't have to understand it, just accept it."

He blows out a gust of air and looks around the bookshop, small, cramped, cluttered, and glorious. His gaze finally lands on me. "I suppose I'll have to, huh?"

My knees go weak as the tension of the last few minutes drains out of me. I slide my arm around Hannah's shoulders and pull her into my side. Her hand comes up to fist the back of my hoodie. I reach for her instinctively, and when I do, she's there reaching back.

"It's up to you, Dad. Just know this is me. This is the life I'm choosing. You can be a part of it or not, but I won't change who I am to please you anymore."

He shakes his head. "I didn't realize I was— Fine. I'll back off. It's your life, and you do what you see fit."

"Thank you."

"But you call your mother and come home for a visit this summer."

I nod. "I will."

He looks miserable and supremely uncomfortable with

so much almost-emotion in the air. "I should get back. I have a meeting in Carlton, down the highway from here, and the roads are bad."

"Sure."

He looks at Hannah again, the condescending judgment gone from his eyes, replaced with what might be respect. He's learning—like I already have—to never underestimate her. "Nice to meet you, Hannah."

"It's nice to meet you, too, Mr. Fisher." She's lying through her teeth, of course, but unlike my father, she's polite.

"We'll see you in Columbus soon, Ben?"

I nod and then he's gone, the bell over the door tinkling in the wake of his exit.

"Jesus, Ben," Alex finally says. "My stepdad can be a judgmental prick, but your dad wins the prize. That was epic."

"I'm really sorry about that, guys. Thank you for everything you said. All of you." I look at Alex and Adele in turn, saving Hannah for last.

"No sweat, Ben," Alex says. "Thanks for the floor show during my break. That was the most entertaining thing to happen on Charles Street in *weeks*. I gotta go, though." She heads for the door but glances back at Hannah and smiles. "Nice to see you around here again, Hannah."

Hannah smiles awkwardly. "Nice to be back."

Adele pats me on the shoulder. "He'll come around, or he won't. But you've got a family either way."

She's right— This store, these people, are my home and family, and they always will be, no matter where I work. I wasn't born into it, but I found it for myself. And I didn't really know how important any of this was to me until I had to fight to keep it.

Adele disappears up the stairs to the loft, and I finally—*finally*—turn back to Hannah. "Where were we?"

She laughs. "Oh, God, that was awful. I told off your *father*. That was an excellent first impression." She claps her hands over her reddening face, but I pull them away.

"Stop it. You were brilliant. And I can't…" I shake my head. "I can't believe you said those things about me. Especially after everything that's happened."

She runs her hands up my arms to my shoulders. "Everything I said was true. I always knew it. Now you do, too."

"Because of you."

She shakes her head. "You did this on your own."

"Because you put me on the right path."

"It goes both ways." Her fingers play with the hair at the nape of my neck, and I lace my hands at the small of her back. "You put me on the right path, too."

This right here—holding someone beautiful and strong who loves me, surrounded by stories within stories—this is all I could ever ask for. I'll never risk losing this again.

"What do you say we try going the rest of the way together?" I say.

Her blue eyes sparkle, and her smile makes me glow from the inside out. When she speaks, her voice is soft and thick with emotion. "I'd say that sounds like the best story of all."

Chapter Thirty-Two

HANNAH

It's Saturday afternoon, and brilliantly sunny outside. Sunlight pours through the front windows of Prometheus, warming it up like a greenhouse inside. Adele is in the back re-doing the psychology shelves, and Alex is here, fresh from her Oasis hot chocolate run. Now she's up front, happily ensconced in some Dan Brown book that made Ben roll his eyes.

She's got a really nice new guy, unlike all the losers she's dated before. I don't know how someone as beautiful and smart as Alex can be such a disaster where men are concerned, but she swears she's got a radar for the walking time bombs. The new guy is coming to pick her up after work. She wants me to meet him, in case she's missing the douchebag signs again.

But for now, I'm glaring at the computer terminal with

Jasmine hovering over my shoulder.

"I don't understand why you have to enter it there if you already recorded the sale," she gripes.

"Because it doesn't show up in inventory if you don't," I explain.

"You know you could just link those databases, right?"

I glance at her. "You can?"

Jasmine rolls her eyes. "Retail 101. Here, let me see." She navigates back to Settings, and within minutes, she's reconfigured the system. "There. Now when you enter a sale, it automatically adjusts the inventory program. We're going to need to streamline this system once the website is up and running."

So after some convincing, I took Ben's old job at Prometheus. At first I wasn't sure— I mean, who am I to work in a bookstore? Before Ben handed me that first book last fall, I didn't even read for fun. I could never do for someone what Ben did for me. But he said most people who wander into bookstores have come there because they already love to read. I don't need to save anyone's life through literature— I just need to learn the stock and ring up sales. And it means I get to spend my free time here at Prometheus, which is hardly like working at all.

The first time Jasmine visited me at work, she was horrified by Ralph's antiquated business practices. Now she's determined to drag Prometheus into the twentieth century. She signed up for a special seminar in advanced business models in the fall, and for her final project, she's building a website for the store.

But that's three months away. Spring semester is over, and she's headed home. She only stopped over to say good-bye before she and Sean head back to Akron. I'm going to miss the hell out of her this summer, but it's only for a few months, since we've decided to get an apartment together off campus next year.

The bell over the door tinkles, and Ben and John come into the store. We're all headed to the movies, but John's got plans later, so Ben and I will be on our own for our last night before I go home. I'm only home for a week, though, before I come back for the summer session. I'm taking a few classes, still exploring my options. Plus, now I have my job at Prometheus.

Ben is staying in Arlington for the summer, too, working his ass off at World of Books. He's been there two months, and they've already made him an assistant manager. He doesn't love wearing the dumb red polo shirt every day, but sometimes I stop in to surprise him. I almost always find him dragging some stunned customer through the store, that light gleaming in his eyes as he talks about every great book they pass. He's found a way to make it work for him, even there.

Ben crosses to the register and leans across the counter to kiss me. "Hey."

"Hey, yourself." I grab him by the back of the neck and pull him in for another kiss.

"Okay, break it up, kids," John says over Ben's shoulder.

I giggle. "All right, we'll save it for later."

"After I'm gone, please," John says. "Hey, Commander Jasmine."

Jasmine scowls at him. They don't exactly get along. "Hey, Slacker John," she quips.

"Corporate domination looks good on you, Commander

J."

She runs a scathing glance over his messy hair, wrinkled plaid shirt, and faded jeans. "Slacker PhD Candidate suits you, too."

John chuckles and shakes his head.

"Okay," Jasmine says. "Sean's waiting. I gotta go."

I sigh. "So this is it?"

"Until September."

She pulls me into a ferocious hug. Jasmine's hugs are nearly a punishment. "Girl, I'm going to miss the hell out of you."

"Me, too. Call me, okay? I want to know how your internship is going." Jasmine's spending the summer with her grandmother in Chicago because she landed herself an internship with the manager of the Four Seasons Hotel. They didn't even have an internship program, but she tracked down the manager's email and talked him into creating one just for her. I wouldn't expect any less from her.

Ben hugs Jasmine good-bye. She finally decided, despite our rocky start, that she likes him. John makes like he's going in for a hug, too, and busts up laughing at her horrified expression. "Catch you in the fall, Commander J," he calls as she leaves.

I watch her leave Prometheus with a lump in my throat. When I get back to our room tomorrow morning, she'll be gone and the year really will be over. It's so bittersweet that it makes my heart hurt for a moment. Then Ben slides his arm around my shoulders and smiles at me, his eyes shining behind his glasses, and all I feel is the sweet. The bitter was worth it.

Much later that night, after the movie and dinner, John leaves for Smitty's, and Ben and I climb into his bed. Wrapped in sheets, skin on skin, as close as we can get, Ben presses kisses against my shoulder, arm, collarbone, the hollow at the base of my neck.

"It's just a little over two hours to Cleveland," he murmurs. "Maybe I could come up on Sunday. World of Books closes early on Sunday."

"But you have to open the store on Monday."

"Not till eleven. I'd see you. I could kiss you."

"My dad likes you, but he won't let you sleep in my room. *This*" — I kiss him to punctuate my point — "won't happen."

"I don't care. I'll drive up just so I can kiss you good night on your front porch, and then I'll drive back."

I giggle, partly at his dramatic declarations and partly because his kisses tickle my neck. "Don't be silly. It's only a week, and then I'll be back in the summer resident dorms."

Ben chuckles. "If you think you're spending a single night in those summer resident dorms, you're crazy."

"What do you mean?"

"John's going to be in Arizona for six weeks doing that observatory thing."

The implication sinks in slowly. "We'll have your apartment to ourselves?"

"Every night."

I flush. *Every* night? "Oh…um…"

"You can keep a toothbrush at the summer dorm if it makes you feel better," he says. "But I want you here with me." His grin is wide and infectious. I might explode from happiness this summer, Ben and me together like this every night. I run my thumb over his bottom lip.

"I changed my mind," I whisper. "Drive up on Sunday, just so you can kiss me good night."

"I will, I promise."

"Except you have to go see your parents, too."

Ben sighs and buries his face into a pillow. I feel bad reminding him, but it's important for him to keep trying to repair things with them. He's talked to them once or twice on the phone, stilted, awkward conversations that didn't last longer than ten minutes. Still, it's Ben's family. One day they won't be so disappointed in his choice, and when that day comes, I want them to still be speaking, so Ben can see it for himself.

"I'd rather come see you."

"I'd rather you come see me, too. But you need to see them. And once I'm back in Arlington, I won't want to let you go."

He kisses my shoulder, the side of my neck, my cheek, and the corner of my mouth. "I love you."

"I know."

"I can't imagine ever loving someone else the way I love you."

My eyes water. "I know." And I feel the same way— This just feels so right. There will never be a more right person, a more right love than this one.

"We can't promise forever just yet." He brushes a strand of hair out of my eyes.

"Not yet."

He chuckles. "I mean, I can't promise I can afford

groceries next week, so big life commitments should probably wait. But I promise one day I *will* promise you forever. I'll change your life, Hannah."

I hold his face in my hands, full of all the love bubbling up in me. "You already have."

The End

Acknowledgments

A year and a half ago, I was on a business trip in a college town that will remain unnamed. On my morning off, I took a stroll through the charming downtown district and found my way into a great used bookstore. As I browsed, a college boy in glasses came in, slipped behind the counter, plugged his iPod into the store sound system, and started his shift. I hopped on twitter and described the scene, which felt like the opening of a romance novel. My timeline thought it would make a good book, too. I kept waiting for the heroine to enter and the scene to begin, so on my flight home, I started outlining the story, which became *This Book Will Change Your Life*.

Many thanks to my encouraging friends on twitter, that lovely college town, that magical used bookstore, and that boy in glasses who has no idea that he sparked a novel when he came to work that day.

I owe a tremendous debt to Anne Forlines for early

editorial feedback and support. Many thanks as well to Jennifer deSylva, Sara Mizzen, and Denise Cataudella for pre-reading, feedback, and prosecco. Always prosecco.

Thank you to Stephen Morgan, my fantastic editor at Entangled. Working on this book with him has been such an amazing experience!

About the Author

Amanda has loved romance novels since she read that very first Kathleen E. Woodiwiss novel at fifteen. After a long detour into a career as a costume designer in theatre, she's found her way back to romance, this time as a writer.

A native Floridian, Amanda transplanted to New York City many years ago and now considers Brooklyn home, along with her husband, daughter, two cats, and nowhere near enough space.

http://www.amandaweavernovels.com
@AWeaverWrites
Facebook
Newsletter